THE
LAST
SACRIFICE

ROBERT T. ESTORGA

BALBOA.PRESS

A DIVISION OF HAY HOUSE

Balboa Press books may be ordered through booksellers or by contacting:

Balboa Press
A Division of Hay House
1663 Liberty Drive
Bloomington, IN 47403
www.balboapress.com
844-682-1282

Print information available on the last page.

ISBN: 978-1-5043-8499-5 (sc)
ISBN: 978-1-5043-8500-8 (e)

Balboa Press rev. date: 10/23/2023

THE UNTOLD CRUCIFIXION STORY

The Greatest Coverup in History

During the crucifixion, a flurry of multifaceted messages were unleashed, amidst a number of physical and prophetic signs. Beginning with Pontius Pilate's declaration nailed above the cross, all were delivered by a grieving Father as He watched His only begotten Son being crucified. Among these messages were the proclamations that Jesus was the awaited Messiah, and God Himself!

So what happened? Where are these messages?

The answer begins with the chief priests and what they saw embedded within Pilate's sign. To their astonishment, it was the tetragrammaton revealing God's name – **YHVH**.

To the chief priests, the shock of seeing the name of YHVH above the cross would have sent a poignant parallel to the practice of tagging the chosen Passover lamb, especially since it was also meant to identify the sinful owner. This would have been theologically mind-blowing! Such a glaring declaration would not only have pointed to Jesus as

YHVH's Passover lamb, but more shockingly, placed God Himself (Genesis 22:8 GNB) as somehow partaking in the consequence of sin (2 Corinthians 5:21 KJV)!

So overwhelming and utterly unacceptable was this notion that the chief priests demanded that Pilate change his sign (John 19:19-21 KJV). *Interestingly, the change protested for was at the very spot that defined the tetragrammaton!*

Oh yes, another reason for the chief priest's demand for Pilate to change what he had written was that the sacred tetragrammaton, **YHVH**, *when placed above the cross*, translates:

Behold the hand! Behold the nail!

These learned priests soon realized that unfolding before them was the culmination of their teachings regarding the coming Messiah.

In retrospect, perhaps it was the stark realization that their teachings had always pointed to Jesus as their Messiah. Perhaps it was the thought of their corrupt reign over Israel coming to an end, or the fear that they had just crucified their Messiah!

In any event they frantically sought to squelch these messages. Soon realizing the futility of such a monumental task, they panicked. In their unrelenting fervor, they somehow managed to compel the nation of Israel to do the unthinkable and *erase its own alphabet!*

So, for almost 2,000 years, the brunt of these messages remained hidden...until now.

Recently, some of **YHVH**'s messages were disclosed by a Rabbi who revised the ancient Hebrew alphabet and reintroduced the symbolic messages and their meaning.

(But this was only the beginning.)

At the noon hour, great earthquakes (as later recorded by Origen) shook the earth. The sun suddenly darkened and went down, while a blood moon rose and 'filled' the sun's now vacated position (as recorded by separate secular writers). In the darkness, terrified eyes found themselves suddenly gazing up at the Taurus Constellation, within which shone the Aldebaran star. To the Jews, Aldebaran symbolized **God**, or *'aleph'* (the first letter of the Hebrew alphabet).

From the beginning, *aleph* also had the distinction of being conjoined with tav, the last letter of the Hebrew alphabet, thus becoming the two-letter word, 'et'. The import of 'et' was apparent to the Old Testament authors who utilized it over 10,000 times. A truly essential word, despite being untranslatable, that is, until the appointed time...until the Crucifixion.

With *aleph*, now hovering in proximity to the cross, the learned chief priests and others would recall the mysterious *aleph/tav* connection and view the 't' shaped cross as now representing *'tav'*. This revelation, with Christ on the cross, would contextually render *'tav'* as **'upon the cross'**.

To the terrified chief priests, the stark proximity of *alephtav* would have delivered the profound implication that Jesus Christ was:

'God upon the Cross'

But this was more than an implication. In the book of Revelation, *aleph* and *tav* are translated as Alpha and Omega. Unfortunately, this obscured the fact that, in Hebrew, Alpha and Omega are actually *aleph vav tav*, with *vav* being 'and'.

From its first appearance, the tetragrammaton, **YHVH** (H*a*Yehudim VeMelech H*a*Nazarei Yeshua), which revealed **"Behold the hand! Behold the nail!"**, also revealed that 'vav' translated as '**nail**'. Thus, when Jesus declares, "I am Alpha and Omega", He is proclaiming, "I am *aleph vav tav*. This declaration of Jesus, at once, becomes a fearsome revelation,

"I am **God nailed upon the cross!"**

And with this, **YHVH** declared, as Jesus once
declared, a wonderous mystery of our triune
God, *"I and my Father are one."* John 10:30 KJV
Also see: Genesis: 22:8 GNB

The Last Sacrifice weaves the most impactful of these messages through a fictionalized action-adventure story. Within this story, I also present evidence detailing the whereabouts and purpose of the Ark of the Covenant. *By the way, there were two, one was a decoy!*

My hope is that the splendor and fullness of God's multi-faceted messages will bring awareness to God's desire in seeking a personal relationship with each of us. Like the Roman Centurion's epiphany, whose conversion meant death to this world, but everlasting hope in the life to come!

To garner fact from fiction, a partial list of facts woven between the two stories is presented. (*Sources can be found in the back of the book*)

1. Researchers lost in Antarctic.
2. Several passageways leading deep into the earth exist, many with claims of alleged spirit/alien inhabitation and enlightenment. One lies beneath the Antarctic.
3. A recent discovery of a city-sized anomaly under a massive frozen lake in the Antarctic.
4. The chromosome count was finally established in 1956.
5. Basement gun ranges in high schools were common and safely operated for decades.
6. Confiscated B-17G – one of four covertly bound for Israel.
7. 2nd 'decoy' Ark (of the Covenant) was the one carried into battle and was never meant for sacrifices.
8. Evidence that the real Ark of the Covenant lies beneath the Crucifixion site exists. Despite the controversy, this evidence addresses every theological proviso written about the Ark's true purpose.
9. Nazis, the occult, and the Aldebaran/Aryan race connection.
10. A B-47 carrying two nukes was presumably lost at sea and never found. (March 10, 1956)
11. At Christ's death, a 4-fold message was instantly *'delivered'* with the 'renting' of the Temple veil (*Wow!*)
12. The 3 hours of darkness, which occurred at the time of the Crucifixion, was a universal event documented by both Christ's followers and secular historians. (Yes, *universal!!!*)

13. A week after the war with Germany, the submarine U-234 surrendered. Among her cargo were found ten canisters of uranium oxide bound for Japan. (*Used in the making of atomic bombs*)
14. Saint Martin de Porres feast day is Nov.3.
15. Somatids (Microzymas) discovered by Dr. Pierre Jacques Antoine Bechamp.
16. Some 'useful' Nazis found guilty at the Nuremberg trials were released and returned to their positions in the pharmaceutical cartel, a cartel condemned for war crimes!
17. Nazis were gathered by the U.S. (including rocket scientists) after the war - Operation Paperclip
18. Nazi saboteurs – Operation Pastorius
19. In 1979, an aging nuclear detection satellite recorded a nuclear blast on or near Antarctica. Despite the evidence, the U.S. denied the incident.
20. NASA's 1st stellar traveler, Pioneer 10, is heading towards the Aldebaran star system. *Who at NASA chose a destination that figured so prominently in Nazi ideology?*

CHAPTER 1

❖

September 1, 1979
SECRET BASE, ANTARCTICA

B ONE-CHILLING WINDS SWEEP through a broad ravine in
Antarctica. Braving the elements, a C-130's ground
crew hurries to finish their pre-flight duties. One crewman
rushes out from under the massive plane and signals the
pilots to fire up the engines. Snow tractors race between
dome-shaped barracks teeming with activity. In a corner
office, seasoned senior NSA agent De Niro sits. Bound for
home, he slowly packs. Sadly, for De Niro, what should have
been an exhilarating time, instead carries a burden of guilt
and regret. He pauses to flex his arthritic hands. A week has
passed since his wife's last call. Why hadn't he answered the
phone? Now, one day away from heading home and his gaze
again falls upon the government letter informing him of
his wife and son's tragic death. He slowly resumes packing.

Suddenly, klaxons begin to blare. Rousing the base to
life, it sends crewmen scrambling in all directions. Nearby,
the C-130 taxies onto a makeshift tarmac. The engine's
roar beckons the old 'war horse' in De Niro. He resists the
impulse, but when a scant rescue team speeds past, it's all

the impetus the 30-year veteran needs. He begins reloading his rescue backpack.

Hurrying past, the base commander stops and leans in to voice his objection. "And just where do you think you're going?" An awkward moment of silence spurs the commander to quickly add his condolences, "Sorry, about… If there's anything—"

"You're short-handed." De Niro continues to pack. "This one's on the house."

The commander senses this might be good for De Niro and nods before rushing off. As De Niro checks his equipment, he hesitates at the one piece he hopes he never needs. It's the only piece with a picture of his family that he'd put there almost a year ago. He closes his eyes and says a prayer as he stuffs it into his jacket.

The huge C-130 races down the runway. On board, the rescue team, comprised of just two heavily armed soldiers and another, younger NSA agent, are aware of De Niro's tragic loss and are surprised to see him. They remain cordial but silent.

For De Niro, the adrenalin rush of an emergency search and rescue provides a much-needed distraction. But he soon finds that with every passing minute comes a memory, and with every memory, troubling guilt. The massive C-130 suddenly surges forward, as if to remind him that lives are at stake.

Barely an hour in and an uneasiness wears on all. They slowly gather around the young NSA agent who sits at a dedicated screen. As if on cue, a faint beep quickly breaks the tension, bringing smiles of relief. Their training kicks in as they quickly rehearse emergency extraction procedures. De Nero's uneasiness is heightened. He alone realizes that the signal emanates from a forbidden zone.

He quietly murmurs, "*So, it's finally happened. God help us.*"

Both pilots tense as they grip the controls and descend into the blanketing fog. Hearts pound as all strain to see through the blinding cloud cover.

The fog parts, exposing the frozen wasteland, only feet away and rising fast. Instinctively, all stumble back and brace for impact. The rising tundra suddenly falls away, plunging their view over a cliff and onto a frozen installation, bordering a vast frozen lake. The pilots circle the area once before landing.

The huge C-130 sits at the end of a frozen runway with engines on high idle, ready for a quick escape. The two riflemen secure a perimeter, oblivious to a thin green mist that lingers waist high. De Niro remains quiet as he and the young NSA agent don protective gear. Emerging, they scan the area and quickly pinpoint a faint signal emanating from a distant, lone shack, atop the frozen lake.

Both spy a body protruding from the doorway and double-time it. Adrenaline takes over as fear suddenly grips both men who realize the mounds of snow they're rushing past are frozen bodies. They focus and press on.

The pilots and riflemen watch intently, unaware of the grisly discovery. They are also unaware of the green mist as it snakes its way up the front landing gear.

The agents cautiously approach the lone shack and begin taking pictures. They give the dead researcher a quick once-over, keenly noting that he grips a spent sidearm. Being careful not to disturb his remains, they step over the frozen body and enter the small shack. Among the stacks of frozen equipment, a sonar ping is heard as one screen reports. A signal emanates from far below their position, prompting them to look for a way down. Both suddenly gaze in horror at a blood-stained, cylindrical elevator.

With hearts pounding, they check their sidearms and begin their descent, deep into the frozen lake. The cramped quarters and blood-stained walls bring the young agent close to a claustrophobic panic.

They emerge through a domed ceiling, far above charred city ruins, cleverly built upon a steaming geothermal lake. The nightmarish scene of desolation and an eerie green glow have both struggling to control their fears as they quickly snap photographs and take air samples.

De Niro's eyes are drawn to a huge, cavernous opening to their right. Chills suddenly chase the sweat running down his back. Fearful of saying a word, he nudges the new agent. Turning, the agent inadvertently bumps a tool left on the elevator floor. The long fall ends in a splash, shattering the silence.

Within the cave, panicked but hopeful eyes open. A wounded researcher frantically hobbles out. From deep within the cavern, a howling grows as the ground shakes. The agent's startled movements cause him to look up. In desperation, the terror-stricken researcher draws a deep, rasping breath and shouts, "RUN!"

Scores of human-like creatures emerge grunting and panting. Many have deep gashes and charred flesh, while others are covered in oozing blisters. As they charge from the cavern, some in tattered uniforms stop and surround the researcher. With savagery, they pounce.

The young agents freezes in horror as De Niro quickly slaps the up button. The gathering hordes quickly merge to form a living ladder in a frenzied attempt to reach the dangling elevator cables. The elevator strains under the increasing load. Finally surfacing, both agents bound from the elevator. To buy time, De Niro punches the down button. With a whoosh, the elevator plummets.

The agents dart from the shack, frantically signaling for takeoff. Agonized shrieks pierce the twilight sky as throngs begin pouring out of the shack. The startled riflemen spring into action, sending a volley of automatic fire before lobbing grenades as they retreat. A brief silence occurs when the first wave of creatures are driven back. Suddenly, the shack explodes as a surging mass of creatures race to cover the runway. Slamming the C-130's hatch shut, De Niro races to the cockpit door and pounds.

"*Go, go, go!*" De Niro shouts.

Both pilots, blistered and profusely sweating from exposure to the mysterious green mist, see that the runway is overrun. In a weakened state, they struggle to turn the C-130 onto the frozen lake.

With engines at full throttle, the C-130 rolls forward. Skidding and bouncing on the uneven ice, the pilots now battle against constant overcorrecting as they fight to gain traction. The rough ride causes one rifleman to be tossed, landing him face-down on a jumbled pile of cables.

Seeing the creatures racing towards them, the co-pilot reaches down in anticipation of the pilot's signal.

"Not...yet!" The pilot gasps as his lungs begin to fill with fluid. "Fire flares."

The co-pilot hits the countermeasures, sending clusters of flares flying. The white-hot flares strike, burning deep into the terrified creatures. Others quickly replace the fallen and reach the plane just as it begins to accelerate.

The pilot draws a deep rasping breath. "Now!"

Immediately, the co-pilot hits the rocket assist take-off system. Returning to the controls, both he and the pilot pull back, lifting the huge C-130 skyward. The rifleman, still clinging to the cables, slides to the back of the plane.

Smoke from the rockets disorients the creatures, causing them to run headlong into the flames. Some blindly catapult themselves. One overshoots. Striking a propeller, both the creature and propeller explode, hurling shrapnel and tissue in all directions. The pilot quickly shuts down the port-side, outboard engine.

Just as the huge aircraft lifts, the largest of the creatures leaps. With arms extended, it grabs onto the C-130's tail. Scurrying across the fuselage, the creature hops onto the wing and begins tearing a hole behind the port, inboard engine.

The new agent watches in horror as the creature shreds the metal cowling as if it were made of cardboard. The rifleman takes aim thru a doorway, but the creature quickly disappears into the wing. In shock, the soldier looks back at the now terrified junior agent who quickly draws his sidearm and looks all about in frightened anticipation.

As the other soldier struggles to lift himself from the mound of cables, he hears a metallic click as something drop. He grabs his chest and realizes a live grenade has tumbled down thru the cables. He frantically thrusts his hand into the cables, but the grenade explodes. Both soldier and cables are violently sucked through the jagged, port-side blast hole. A frigid, howling wind swiftly fills the plane.

The engine damaged by the creature suddenly explodes, sending shrapnel tearing through the fuselage. The plane shudders and banks left. All hold on as the pilots fight to keep the giant plane from rolling.

The terrified agent glances over at De Niro who is calmly lighting a cigarette.

The young agent turns to find the creature now at the doorway. Before he can warn the rifleman, it strikes, digging its talons into his neck. The hapless rifleman struggles while the creature uses its other claw to climb in. The rifleman is tossed out of the plane.

Lights flicker as the creature slowly advances on the horrified junior agent who yells while fiercely emptying his sidearm. Every round strikes with ghastly effect. The mangled creature pounces, strangling the flailing young agent. It is soon over as both die in a grotesque heap.

Agent De Niro calmly puts his hand inside his jacket and waits.

He watches in stunned amazement as a winged, transparent spirit rises from the dead creature and approaches to within inches. Defiantly, De Niro blows smoke in its face, revealing a hideous form.

Recoiling, it drifts back as De Niro gently pulls a detonation switch from his jacket. The furious spirit turns a crimson red. With a hellish shriek, it charges. De Niro longingly caresses the snapshot of his family as he moves his thumb over a pulsing red button. The raging demon is inches from striking when there is a brilliant flash, followed by a thunderous shockwave. Within the flaming debris, smoke outlines the flurry of wings beating rhythmically.

CHAPTER 2

❖

October 29, 1956
(23 years earlier)

WITH ONLY MINUTES to the bell, retired cartographer-turned-archeologist-turned-teacher, Zachary 'Zac' Gomes impatiently drums his fingers steadily upon a package brought to his desk.

"Where was I? Ah, good question. Yes, earlier this year, researchers managed to finally determine the human chromosome count to be 46."

While Professor Gomes responds, everyone begins shuffling in anticipation of the bell.

Zac speaks louder, "This discovery will make it easier to follow the biological journey of our ancient ancestors prior to their becoming...our ancient ancestors. Anyway—"

Zac is interrupted by a slow-rising hand. He mumbles, *"Another question, my lucky day."* The anxious student stammers, "Will they—"

Zac returns the interruption with a tap to his temple.

"Sorry." The student quickly removes his hat. "You were saying they...uh, chromosomes, can tell who...uh, the father was, or is...of a person...who is? I mean, was?"

Zac notices several nervous male students and one wide-eyed, gum-popping, and very pregnant female. He indulges in some cruel fun.

"Oh, yes, authorities, I mean researchers, with this new discovery, can precisely tell who the father is...uh...or was." He capitalizes on student habitats as he paces. "Now, by utilizing chromosomes, we can track and identify the wild, wanton, and irresponsible activities of our ancestors. With the slightest bit of physical evidence, left, say, in the back seat of a chariot, under ancient coliseum bleachers..." Zac's mind wanders as he unwittingly adds his own youthful indiscretions, "In a museum, floating down the Nile..."

Zac suddenly realizes what he's doing but the male students are lost in their own haunting memories.

They squirm as Zac eagerly focuses on each boy's prominent features.

An approaching storm grows louder as Zac slowly paces down an aisle.

"Yes, chromosomes should easily reveal the telltale features of a nose, the eyes, ears." Zac stops and focuses on one student. "Or high cheekbones." Zac is really getting into it. "In fact, I'm sure this discovery will make catching, I mean, identifying those elusive ancestors much easier."

Some nervously look away and others just stare straight ahead. Zac smirks as he looks down at one student. "There will be no escape."

The room grows quiet as the lightning and thunder intensify. The male students remain lost in fearful recollection, while the pregnant female chews faster and gazes straight ahead. Nervous stomachs churn. Zac quietly picks up a yardstick. The spirited slap to his desk is unexpectedly followed by a huge thunderclap. Amid startled gasps, the bell mercifully rings.

9

Above the din of jostling and the mad rush, Zac strains to be heard, "Remember your essays!"

The class noisily bemoans their fate as they leave.

Zac impatiently attempts a bit of encouragement. "C'mon people, it's your family tree. How hard can it be? Points for originality are built in."

The class moans louder.

Zac counters, "Hey, what'd I say about any negative behavior towards—" Zac is silenced as he turns to see the University's Dean approaching, dodging students as they file past.

"No!" Zac unwittingly sets a bad example.

The Dean sighs, "Now Dr. Gomes, we weren't going to forget our photo session... Not again?"

Bemoaning his fate, Zac tucks his package under his arm and is insistent, "No, really, I can't—"

"Afford to miss it?" Dean Carlyle interrupts. "I agree! It'll only take a minute and it's great publicity for the University. Let's go... C'mon!"

A bevy of flashing cameras vies to capture the moment. Zac attempts to leave when a scholarly-looking chap grabs his hand with a vigorous handshake, causing Zac to almost drop his package.

"Professor, we're sorry you couldn't make the presentation...but, again, from the society, our heartfelt congratulations and in recognition of your dedication and contributions to archeology. Oh, and if I'm not mistaken, to your earlier discovery of the Ark of the Covenant."

"That was so long ago, almost ancient history itself." Everybody laughs as Zac quickly interjects, "But that wasn't me." The noisy crowd forces Zac to shout, "Name's Gomes, Zachary Gomes, not—." frustrated, he stops.

Seeing Zac heading towards the door, the Dean shouts, "Wait, you have other visitors."

"No, I'm late!"

An exasperated Dean exclaims, "And exactly what am I to do with them?"

Zac's sarcasm gets the best of him. "I don't know, take their picture, see what develops."

CHAPTER 3

Z AC HURRIES UP the stairs of a nearby high school just as the final bell rings and the last of the students eagerly make their escape. Still clinging to his package, he glances at hastily scribbled instructions as he quickly moves through an empty hallway.

Suddenly, muffled gunfire echoes from a downstairs corridor. He backtracks and picks up his pace. More shots ring out. Racing down the dimly lit staircase, Zac swings a door open but is abruptly stopped by a rifle barrel, shoved against the side of his nose. He slowly moves the barrel away to see a Boy Scout elevated on some bleachers and cleaning his rifle.

"Sorry, sir!" The startled scout is apologetic as he quickly retracts his rifle.

Zac takes a deep breath. "I'm your substitute."

A burly man in flight coveralls quickly approaches, barking orders, "Cease fire!" The scouts deftly unload and bench their firearms.

The tall figure emerges from the shadows and eagerly extends a hand to Zac. "Wow, Dr. Gomes, Captain Nick Desmond. This is a real honor."

Zac is jostled by the Captain's energetic handshake but manages to politely insist, "Please, call me Zac."

"Sure thing, call me Nick."

As Zac surveys the room, he jokingly remarks, "I didn't know they had captains in the scouts."

Zac's attempt at humor seems lost as Nick remarks, "I'm stationed at the airbase with Abe. He asked me to sub while he tends to his wife and new son."

"A boy, that's great." Zac is happily surprised. "I guess Abe forgot he'd asked me to—"

"Excuse me!" Nick turns to instruct the class. "Collect your casings."

He turns back to Zac who comments, "Look, I can see you're pretty busy."

Nick shrugs. "Yeah, anyway, I was with Abe when he got the call. You never saw anyone so excited. He asked me to help out."

"I got that."

"Sorry, Abe was really excited."

Zac is eager to leave. "Sure, look, if you won't be needing me, Nick, nice meeting you."

As Zac starts out, an overly anxious Nick suddenly blocks his escape. "One moment, please!"

Nick turns towards the young scouts and smiles. "Okay, whoever wants to earn their brain freeze merit badge, follow me to the soda parlor across the street."

The Boy Scouts are elated and begin chanting, "Ice cream, ice cream, ice cream!"

Nick turns back to Zac and shouts over the chant, "I have something for you, from Abe. I'll swing by later with it, if you don't mind!"

Zac is caught off guard, but what can he say? "Yeah, sure."

As Zac leaves, he shakes his head and smiles at the energetic scouts who begin jumping in unison.

CHAPTER 4

A CAR QUIETLY ROLLS up to Zac's house just as the approaching storm arrives, unleashing its fury.

Zac carefully arranges student papers around a steaming TV dinner strategically placed before the TV, switched on but with the volume off. Easing into a long night, Zac can't help but gaze over at the package he has been reluctantly guarding as it rests on the coffee table. A knock on the door disrupts his quiet sanctuary.

Opening the door, he can barely see through the deluge until lightning backlights an imposing silhouette. Hidden in front of the tall shadowy figure, stands Professor Jacob Malkin, an old friend of the family. Suddenly, Zac hears a cheerful quip.

"Hello, Zacky!"

As a grinning Jacob slowly emerges, Zac is filled with mixed feelings. Sensing an immediate tension, Jacob quickly adds, "Uh, your father said you'd get a kick... Anyway, to the point, I, uh, that is, we sent you a package for safe-keeping."

Annoyed, Zac fires back, "Should've known! The two of you? Well, what's the big secret this time?"

Jacob stammers, "Yes, well, if I—"

"And where is dear ol' dad?" Zac turns away. "No, I don't want to know. Is he in trouble again? Don't tell me! He'll be the death of me yet."

Jacob fires back, "Now, just you wait." Jacob and his assistant follow Zac in. "He thought you would, more than anyone, appreciate our discovery. Since an Ark was found, perhaps you might—"

"An Ark...?" Zac stammers, "...of the Covenant?" He suddenly becomes adamant. "There is only one Ark of the Covenant!"

Jacob concedes, "Well, yes but... Well, Zac, there is something you should know."

Zac snaps, "About what? Make sense. No, I'm busy... Okay, what is it?"

Jacob sees his precious package and hurries a response as he hastily moves towards it, "My assistant, Mr. Beck... sorry, this is my assistant, Mr. Beck. He can answer any questions. Now, if you will excuse me."

Jacob eagerly grabs his package and sits as Beck explains, "Yes, the Professor and I believe he has discovered what may be the most challenging and provocative secret of the ancient world."

Beck's German accent raises the hair on Zac's neck. A lingering reflex from the war, Zac suppresses his unwarranted prejudice. Jacob mumbles something in Hebrew, causing both Zac and Beck to turn their heads.

Zac steps towards Jacob. "Wait! You...you and dad, you're the ones?"

Jacob is euphoric and doesn't hear Zac. "Magnificent! The blood... The count. Zac, the chromosome count, Zac, it's..." Jacob's words trail as he looks up to see Beck pointing a German luger.

"Rather unique?" Beck becomes insolent as he interrupts Jacob in midsentence. "So, it's true. Well, I haven't the time. If you would Professor... The papers."

Zac slowly moves towards Beck who quickly reacts and motions Zac back towards Jacob.

As Jacob extends the papers, a knock on the door startles Beck. Zac reacts, slapping the luger out of Beck's hand while driving his fist upwards, hitting Beck hard, but to no effect. Beck retaliates by delivering a stunning blow. Before Zac can shake it off, Beck grabs him with one arm and propels Zac across the room.

Just then, there's another, louder knock on the door. Beck snatches the papers and rushes out the back door and into the storming night. Zac gives chase but stops at the door and peers into the darkness. Jacob quickly follows, his pace slowing as he approaches Zac.

Lightning illuminates Jacob as he stands in the shadows. The storm has become eerily silent, as if waiting for Jacob to speak, "The blood...is from the Ark." Thunder punctuates Jacob's proclamation.

A flash of lightning illuminates Zac who is momentarily overwhelmed. "It was you? Where...? How...?"

Jacob begins to explain, "The chromosome count—"

"From sacrifices?" Zac snaps as he turns. "Why would you...?" Suddenly, Zac is unable to accept what he's now thinking. "No, it can't be." Zac becomes insistent. "Where is it? Do you know what you're saying?"

"Would that I could." Overwhelmed by Zac's rapid queries, Jacob sarcastically fires back.

"Don't!" Zac sternly states.

"The blood doesn't lie." Jacob insists.

Facing the darkness, Zac pauses before quietly asking, "What exactly are you saying?"

The wind picks up as Zac again turns towards Jacob who matter-of-factly, states, "The Ark that was earlier found... was a decoy."

Zac finally hears Nick's pounding and yelling, "Professor Zac! Are you alright?"

Disheveled and tending a bloodied lip, Zac opens the door. Nick spots Jacob but gazes at Zac's tousled appearance.

"Wow! I love parties!"

Drawing his handkerchief, Zac gingerly touches his cut lip. "Good timing. I thought I said to call me Zac."

"I did." Nick smiles while surveying the room. "Hey, did you throw the party, or did the party throw you?"

"Listen to me!" A frantic Jacob speaks out. "Beck will try contacting his people. As it is, they're probably waiting for him, as we speak!"

Nick asks, "Who's Beck?"

Jacob laments, "A colleague, or so I thought." Jacob turns and sharply warns Zac, "He'll try to catch a flight back!"

Zac demands answers. "What people? Flight back to where?" He winces as he applies pressure to his lip. He looks at Nick, then Jacob, and manages an introduction, "Captain Nick Desmond... Professor Jacob Malkin." Jacob extends his hand.

A slightly hyper Nick thrusts his hand, reciprocating in rapid fashion. "Professor Jacob, pleased to meet you." Continuing his handshake, a slightly hyper Nick quickly asks, "Did you enjoy your time in the desert? You two related?"

Zac grumbles, "Might as well be."

Jacob chuckles, "As a matter of fact—"

"Exactly where is this other Ark?" Zac abruptly interrupts Jacob before quickly turning towards Nick. "And who said anything about the desert?"

Nick looks at Jacob and responds with confidence, "The scent of palm oil, sand on the coat seams, and the Professor's tanned, weathered skin." He is quick to add, "No offense."

Jacob gestures, "None taken."

Nick smiles as he continues, "And the Israeli airline envelope sticking out of the professor's pocket."

"Good heavens!" Jacob had forgotten about the tickets and smiles with confidence as he quickly retrieves the airline envelope from his jacket.

"Tell me those are two-way tickets." Zac sounds with a hopeful insistence.

"Why, yes! Oh, dear!" A distressed Jacob holds open an empty envelope. "Beck!"

"Wait, Israel!" For Zac, it is a stunning revelation. Before anyone says another word, Zac takes control. "Enough!" He looks at Nick and points. "You have something for me, from Abe?"

Nick pulls a blue-banded, metal, cigar-shaped container from his shirt pocket and presents it to Zac who responds, "Thanks."

Jacob cannot contain his concern. "Please, we must get back to Israel, back to the real Ark. It is in grave danger! Beck will take it! He will take it or destroy it!"

Nick casually comments, "Good luck getting there, what with the war and all."

Zac snaps, "War...what war?"

Nick wryly teases, "You guys get out much? Egypt went all high and mighty and took charge of the Suez canal. Anyway, all flights to Israel were canceled except for Israel's own airlines. First come, first serve, I believe." Nick motions with his head towards the silenced TV now displaying news about the Israeli/Sinai war.

Zac's frustration wells up. "This is too much."

A distressed Jacob stumbles back onto a chair, lifting his arms in frustration. "Now what?" As he drops his arms, a hand flops onto a dish of hard candy, much to his delight. While Zac and Nick watch news of the war unfold, Jacob delights in satisfying his sweet tooth.

With the television sound being off, Nick teases Zac who continues to tend his lip, "Are you into lip reading and lip bleeding?" Zac deadpans Nick who apologetically places the blame for his sarcasm. "Sorry, must be the company I keep and way too much ice cream."

A commercial for the upcoming heavyweight match begins. Zac snaps his fingers as he suddenly recalls, "Wait, Abe said you were a tent boxer. You boxed in the Army."

Jacob is intrigued. "Really? I could never get them back in the box. How—"

"Jacob!" Zac tersely interrupts but calmly attempts to clarify, "Circus...tent...boxing."

"Yes... Oh... Really?" Jacob finally gets it.

Nick reluctantly explains, "Okay... Quit flying after the war... Did tent boxing for about a year. Slap your money down, go three rounds with the champ!" Nick solemnly shares a painful memory. "One night, I hit this guy. He never got up... Re-enlisted the next day."

Zac, not keen on consoling, offers what he knows, "Abe said it wasn't your fault, heart attack or something."

A somber Nick nods. "That's what they told his family."

Zac blurts out, "And you were married?"

Nick is suddenly uncomfortable with Zac's questioning. "Abe talks a lot."

Jacob injects his frustration, "Zac, we have to get back."

Zac retorts, "Didn't you hear? There's a war."

Nick picks up and studies the luger as Zac presses Jacob, "Who exactly is this Beck?"

Jacob crunches on another candy while offering a brief recollection, "Don't know really. He and his people arrived the same day Zac's father and I were whisked to an archeological find." Jacob plucks another candy as he continues, "Turned out to be the Ark of the Covenant."

Nick shares a shocking conclusion, "From what you've described, I'd say he's a werewolf."

"A what?" A puzzled Zac queries.

19

Nick quickly adds, "I thought the Ark was already discovered?"

Zac glares at Jacob.

"What will we do?" Jacob laments. "We must get to Israel before Beck. The Ark of the Covenant is the most important of all relics."

Zac looks at Nick, then Jacob, as both look at him. Nick offers a solution, "I have a plane."

Zac shakes his head and gestures. "Not a chance. I have class."

Nick takes offense. "Are you insulting my plane?" Zac again deadpans Nick.

Jacob persists, "Zac, it's the Ark!" Zac raises a cautionary finger toward Jacob.

Nick advises, "Pack light." Zac turns towards Nick and raises a second finger.

"Two minutes." Zac concedes. The exhilaration of such a discovery is just too much to resist.

CHAPTER 5

N ICK'S CREDENTIALS PROMPT quick salutes from the guards at the gate. Driving onto the tarmac makes both Jacob and Zac a bit anxious and uncomfortable. Under a heavy downpour, Nick sets a brisk pace. Their impromptu trek quickly leads them to a lone B-47 Stratojet. Zac's eyes widen at the sight of Nick's *plane*, while Jacob clearly displays a boyish exhilaration.

Zac tries to control his uneasiness with a question, "Jacob, tell me about the Ark."

Nick interjects, "There'll be plenty of time for that," He instructs, "Quit gawking and walk like you belong."

Before Nick takes the pilot seat, he introduces a busy Airman, already seated, "Our navigator, Airman 1st Class Mike Popper." Nick leans towards Mike. "Slight change of plans." He begins to explain, "This is a very special trip for Michael."

"Now don't go jinxing' it."

Nick agrees, "Okay, maybe later, anyway, meet Professor Jacob Malkin and Professor Zac Gomes."

Mike is impressed. "Wow, the Ark guy!"

"Why, yes!" A surprised Jacob responds.

"Sorry, no." Zac visually reprimands Jacob who shrugs. Zac tries to explain, "You got it wrong, kid. The name's Gomes, not... Ah, what's the use."

Jacob smiles at Mike. "Pleased to meet you."

Zac quickly follows, "Likewise, Airman Popper."

"Mike will do!" Mike is eager to forgo the formalities.

Zac nods but can't get past how young the Airman looks. "Sure thing, Mike. By the way, how old are you?"

Mike beams as he proclaims, "Twenty-one next month."

Zac smiles and murmurs, "That old?"

Nick gives a final command before take-off, "Alright everybody, sit tight…and try not to scream." Puzzled, Zac and Jacob look at each other. They finish buckling just as the rocket assist take-off drives the B-47 forward, slamming all into their seats. With engines at full power, Nick grins as he pulls back on the controls, sending the mighty Stratojet up and away. Climbing fast, it disappears into the night sky.

At the New York International Airport, security at Israel's El Al terminal is heightened. Beck nervously looks about as passengers begin boarding. One of the last to be seated, he finds himself alongside an elderly Hasidic Jew traveling with his grandson. They are soon airborne. The young boy quickly unbuckles and with youthful fascination, turns and stares at Beck's large stature. The grandfather turns the boy around and nods apologetically. Beck reciprocates with a cold stare.

Flipping on an overhead light, Beck begins reading Jacob's report. Soon annoyed by the grandfather's snoring, he lowers the papers only to find the young boy gazing, apparently waiting for him to notice. Suddenly, a strong jolt of turbulence bounces the boy onto Beck's lap. As he angrily grabs and lifts the boy by the lapels, the grandfather hurriedly snatches the 5-year-old. He spies a tattoo on Beck's wrist, identifying him as a member of the hated Waffen-SS. He freezes in fear as Beck's glare melts into a smile.

Beck offers some chewing gum, seemingly as a gesture of goodwill. The boy snatches a stick and begins chewing as his grandfather slowly takes a piece. Clutching his grandson in his arms, he eases back into his seat. Beck nods agreeably as he stows his papers, then turns and pretends to sleep.

CHAPTER 6

THE B-47 TOUCHES down at a remote airfield in the Azores. Though filled with curiosity, Zac and Jacob say nothing as they follow Nick, who seems to know exactly what he's doing. At least, they hope he does. A ground crew chatters as they finish for the day. Airman Popper remains with the B-47 while Nick, Zac, and Jacob hurry past the bantering ground crew without so much as a puzzled glance their way. Nick guides Zac and Jacob towards a nearby hanger where a B-17G flying fortress rests.

Zac's mind races as he questions Nick in rapid fashion, "Now what, just fly into Israeli airspace in the middle of a war?"

"Not my first choice, but..." Nick stops mid-sentence to point to the B-17G. "You see that?"

Staring straight ahead, Zac remains focused on the B-47, as he continues his rant, "In a U.S. warplane?"

Nick looks at the B-17G and ponders the ramifications, "Oh, that would really be—"

"Exactly!" Zac retorts.

Jacob scolds Zac, "Zac, let the man speak!"

Nick continues as he motions Zac and Jacob to follow, "That flying fortress was on its way to Israel when it was, uh, confiscated. The Israelis will be expecting it."

"Wait, commandeer a confiscated B-17?" Zac exclaims. "Who are you? How do you know these things?"

Nick is flippant with his answer, "Can't you tell by my uniform? I work for the government."

Zac grumbles, "Don't we all."

Jacob shares his concern, "Beck is well on his way by now. Are you certain? I mean, the B-17—"

"B-17G, professor." Nick quickly corrects Jacob. "Lucky for us, all B-17G's were built with extra fuel tanks for long-range missions."

Jacob quietly states, "More and more, I believe less and less in luck."

A confused Nick turns his head towards a musing Zac.

"What?" Zac feels no compulsion to explain *Jacob*.

Nick just shakes his head and motions. "This way, if you please." Nick opens a locker and tosses Jacob and Zac each a cumbersome, wool flight suit.

Jacob quickly begins suiting up, but Zac has questions, "What's with the suits?"

Nick smirks as he dons his suit. "Relax, here's where it gets fun. We're going to be climbing into the polar jet stream again, to boost our airspeed."

"Again? What do you mean, again? You've done this before? Sounds cold, how cold?"

Nick explains, "Uh, below zero, a couple of times during the war, and we were in it on the way over. We made great time. Any more questions?"

"I'm thinking." Zac struggles with his suit.

"Hopefully, we'll get the same results in the B-17G. Relax, you'll be fine. Look, Jacob's done. Professor, how'd you beat us?"

"B-24's." Jacob answers while admiring his flight suit. Nick is impressed but Zac stops and stares at Jacob who reacts, "What? There were missions. We weren't at liberty... Oh, for heaven's sake!"

Nick teases Zac, "Thought you were the adventurous type. Relax, you'll be fine."

Zac has his own concerns. "How cold did you say?"

Finally, on board, Nick squeezes into the pilot seat, then points to the co-pilot seat. "Zac, if you don't mind, I'll need your assistance. It's going to get a little bumpy."

Zac lumbers behind Nick. "Sure, why not? I can barely move in this thing."

Jacob gets comfortable in the flight engineers' compartment behind Zac and Nick.

One by one, the propellers spin as each engine sputters to life. Nick watches the gauges until all engines are droning in unison. He taxies onto the runway before throttling up. Releasing the brake, he and Zac hold on as the B-17 speeds ahead. Pulling back on the controls, all feel the exhilaration as the mighty fortress soars.

Quickly climbing to 10,000 feet, strong turbulence marks their entry into the jet stream. The plane shudders, causing a startled Zac to grip the controls. "Is this where it gets fun?"

Nick is elated. "Stream's really dropped altitude."

"Aren't we a little low for the jet stream?" Zac grumbles as he struggles to maintain his grip while wearing the bulky, government-issued gloves.

"We're in luck, how 'bout that, Professor?" Nick shares his enthusiasm.

"Providence, my good man." Jacob becomes philosophical.

Nick is happy to report, "At least we won't need oxygen." The plane bucks, causing Nick to also tighten his grip on the controls. "Whoa! Got to watch the turbulence. Riding the stream's kind of like surfing."

"Like what?" Zac struggle to hear above the drone of the engines.

"Surfing, ever been to Hawaii?"

Jacob eagerly chimes in, "Oh, yes, it's all the rage on the west coast!"

Zac shakes his head. "Unbelievable! A sport invented by dolphins! What's next, breaching?" Nick and Jacob chuckle as each then quietly contemplates Zac's remark.

Arriving in Israel, deboarding is swift but orderly. Beck quickly disappears. On board, a flight attendant, checking the seats, comes upon the grandfather and boy. Her screams echo throughout the plane.

CHAPTER 7

‹———————♦———————›

THE LIGHT OF dawn sees Nick eager to abandon his wooly flight suit. He hesitates as he realizes an opportunity to prank Zac. With an impish grin, he casually switches on the autopilot then turns to Zac. "Take the controls, I'm gonna lose this suit."

"What?"

"Just hold course!" Nick shouts as he lumbers past.

"I can't—" Turbulence silences Zac's protest. Zac grips the controls and freezes.

Nick eagerly returns. With a chuckle, he switches off the autopilot.

"Not funny."

Zac is last to remove his flight suit. As he dons his hat, a dazzling sunrise draws his attention to the Israeli shoreline in the distance. Meanwhile, Jacob eagerly munches on some cracker rations he's found.

Zac studies the cracker box, wondering how long it's been stowed in the fortress. Tossing it aside, he confronts Jacob, "So, what did you mean, another Ark?"

Jacob talks between chews, "Haven't you read, didn't your father teach you how to use the Bible?"

Zac is almost apologetic, "Look, just because I don't... Really, another Ark?"

Jacob uncorks and sniffs a dusty canteen then washes down his breakfast. Wiping his mouth, he continues, "Really quite simple, God had a plan. The second Ark was to be a decoy. Since the real Ark had been lost, taken really, at least once before, a replica made sense! But a decoy was inevitable. You see—"

"From what I've heard, if that was a decoy, I'd hate to see the original in action." Zac recalls incredible and terrifying stories about the Ark's power.

Jacob explains, "My boy, the Ark of the Covenant's sole purpose was to bring Yeshua, which is salvation, to fruition.

Zac is startled. "Wait, Yeshua…? Yeshua means salvation?"

Jacob nods.

Zac suspiciously queries, "Isn't that…?"

"The Hebrew name for Jesus?" Jacob smiles. "Yes, His name is quite prominent in the Old Testament… Very telling. That fact has been, shall we say, overlooked for—"

"Since the Crucifixion? Who knew?"

"Who didn't? The prophecies fulfilled at the Crucifixion made it unmistakable." Jacob spins in his seat and begins looking for more food rations as he continues, "Anyway, you do know that others were chosen by God to build the Ark of the Covenant and that Moses was later commanded to build the second, decoy Ark?" Jacob delights in finding a bar of chocolate and begins unwrapping it. "Legend has it that those who built the Ark were caught up, into heaven itself, perhaps as a reward, but also to prevent others from utilizing those same skills for pagan worship. In any case, the decoy was never meant for sacrifices."

Zac confidently offers his own brief recollection, "As I recall, the Ark found didn't have any blood on it."

"Oh, for heaven's sake. It's a good thing I'm sitting down." Jacob's frustration with Zac quickly turns instructive.

"Legend has it that when sacrificial blood was sprinkled, it never touched the Ark but was caught up."

Jacob's rant sees Zac attempt a slight redirect, "What about when the Ark was opened? Story is, it was fiercely defended."

Jacob shrugs. "Perhaps it wasn't defended so much as the trespassers were simply punished. Perhaps the decoy remains a decoy. In any event, it stands to reason that both Arks would be guarded."

Zac has heard enough. "Okay, so where is it?"

"The enemies of Israel were constantly digging tunnels. As the Israeli army pursued the invaders, many artifacts were unearthed." Jacob pauses to savor the chocolate bar. Before continuing, he offers some to Zac, who declines. "But your father and I weren't called in until soldiers stumbled upon the chamber containing the original temple treasures including the Ark!" Jacob pauses, momentarily overwhelmed, "Zac, I saw it! I saw the Ark of the Covenant! Mr. Beck was with us. I had no idea he was a Nazi!"

"War's over." Zac casually remarks. "Besides, not everybody with a luger is a Nazi."

Jacob exclaims, "It all makes sense! He was instructing his people just before we left!" Jacob cannot hide his desperation, "Beck cannot be allowed to take the Ark!"

Zac tries to reassure Jacob, "Look, the whole thing would stink Nazis, what with their obsession with ancient religious artifacts, but the war is over, right?"

Nick smiles, enjoying the conversation, with no desire, let alone ability, to spar in such theological banter.

Zac continues, "Right. Anyway, what I don't get is this Beck's strength."

"C'mon Zac, it was just a lucky punch." Nick hollers back, downplaying Zac's claim.

Zac rubs his jaw, "By the way, what did you mean, Beck was a werewolf?"

Bullets suddenly rip through the cockpit, shattering plexiglass, barely missing Nick before punching holes across the fuselage. A diving Egyptian MIG emerges between them and the sun. Nick reacts, frantically pulling the B-17 up, narrowly missing a collision with the MIG as it swings wide for a second pass.

Zac and Jacob hang on as Nick muscles the fortress away. "Where is he?" Nick exclaims.

Zac pops his head up and into the top turret. "He's coming around, behind us."

Delivering full power, Nick sends the engines screaming as he puts the B-17 into a steep dive. Wrestling with the controls, Nick shouts, "Zac, get over here! The clouds... They're all we've got!" Zac hurries back to his seat where both he and Nick struggle against the mighty fortress as it shudders, racing to escape.

Jacob peers from the top turret and sees the MIG align itself with its hapless prey. "He's slowing, he knows he's got us." The MIG roars closer. Jacob shouts. "He's going to fire at point blank range."

Nick loudly laments, "My kingdom for an idea!"

Zac is suddenly inspired. "Jacob, get the suits, put them on the bomb bay doors!"

"*Yes!*" Nick is elated.

Jacob hurries to throw the wool suits onto the bomb bay doors.

Zac leaves his seat and slaps Nick's shoulder. "Keep 'er steady."

The B-17 shudders as Zac looks through the top turret to gauge the MIG's distance. He grabs the flare gun and shouts to Jacob, "Squirt that kerosene on the suits! Get back, get back!" Jacob squirts fluid as Zac yells, "Open the bay doors!" Jacob wrestles his way to the bombardier's station.

The MIG pilot smiles as he puts his finger on the trigger. As the bay doors open, Zac fires a flare into the suits, igniting them just before they're snatched away. The MIG pilot is startled by the animated flaming figures rushing towards him. He banks hard, just missing the burning debris. He buzzes the fortress.

Jacob watches the MIG roar past, close enough for him to report, "Oh, he looks mad. I don't think—"

"It bought us some distance." Nick interrupts. "We're almost there. Zac, Pronto!"

The MIG suddenly throttles-up and momentarily disappears.

Returning the flare gun, Zac notices a Morse code pad and begins sending an SOS.

He shouts, "Jacob, get over here!" Jacob struggles to keep his balance as he makes his way over. Zac quickly grabs Jacob's finger and presses it on the pad, creating a constant tone. Jacob looks puzzled as Zac loudly explains, "Don't move, that tone tells anyone listening, our position!" Zac leans in and sarcastically remarks, "You didn't know that?"

Jacob gets defensive, "I was merely a passenger on a few B-24's. I didn't fly the things!"

Spotting the MIG returning, an anxious Nick yells, "Zac!"

The diving fortress shakes violently as the engines are pushed to their limits. Zac and Nick wrestle mightily against the controls.

Desperate for a kill, a frustrated but determined MIG pilot carefully aligns himself with the B-17. He lets out a sinister laugh as he prepares to fire a rocket.

Suddenly, from dead ahead, two rapidly climbing P-51's burst through the clouds. Tracer bullets zip past the cockpit causing Nick and Zac to instinctively duck. With guns blazing, they roar past the B-17 and hurl headlong towards the MIG, now directly behind the fortress.

Bullets rock the MIG just as it fires, knocking the rocket's trajectory. It skims and scrapes along the B-17's fuselage with an unsettling metal-on-metal grind. Clipping the top turret, it tumbles into an inboard propeller, shattering both to pieces. Nick quickly shuts down the damaged engine as he watches the rocket tumble away before it harmlessly explodes.

The Egyptian MIG begins smoking as it makes a hasty retreat, easily outrunning the prop-driven fighters. The Israeli P-51's zoom up.

Jacob dons the headphones, unsure of what to say, "Shalom, efshar liknot lekha mashke?" (Hebrew: Hello, may I buy you a drink?)

One P-51 pilot yells back, "Americans! Hold course! You are in a war zone! You are not authorized— A drink? Toda... Thank you!"

"My pleasure, drinks all around!" Jacob's exuberance at being rescued goes a little too far.

Hearing Jacob's comment, Nick whips his headphones off. "Oh, boy. Jacob, don't— Oh, boy!"

Through his headphones, Jacob hears a huge cheer. He pops his head through the turret to see that the sky is now filled with planes.

Jacob exclaims, "Sweet Saint Adrian!"

Nick turns. "Who's Saint Adrian?"

Without his headset, Zac is caught unaware of the conversation. "The patron Saint of beer? What's going on?"

A nervous Jacob tries to change the subject. "Nothing. There just...uh, glad to see us. Yes, we're being escorted."

Nick smiles. "What'd I tell you?"

Jacob mumbles, "There goes the inheritance."

"Inheritance?" Zac knows he's missed something.

Jacob nervously chuckles. "Did I say inheritance? I meant intelligence. I was telling Nick, that Morse Code trick... Spot on!"

CHAPTER 8

W ITH ONE ENGINE out, Nick and Zac land the B-17G with a bounce. As it rolls to a stop, a jeep hastily approaches.

Field Commander Gabriel embraces Jacob who tries to hurry things along as plane after plane begins to land. "Ukhal lehakir lekha et—?" (Hebrew: May I introduce—?)

Commander Gabriel places a hand on Jacob's shoulder, stopping him mid-sentence. "My English has much improved, my friend." The commander turns towards Zac and Nick. "Commander Gabriel, at your service." Nick salutes, Zac nods. The commander eagerly shakes Nick's hand. "So, this is Leonard's son? I am sorry—"

"No!" Jacob quickly interrupts as he spies a score of anxious pilots eagerly approaching. He anxiously gestures towards Zac. "This is Leonard's son."

Gabriel nods. "But of course, and I am so sorry. Your father—"

"My father?" Zac looks at Jacob.

"The Ark!" Jacob again interrupts before a puzzled Zac can ask the commander to explain. "My friend, I apologize but it's about the Ark! We believe it may be in great danger!"

Nick sees the smiling pilots eagerly approaching. "Ah! Yes, no time to lose."

"Yes, remember Mr. Beck?" A worried Jacob explains, "We believe he may try to steal the Ark!"

Taken aback, Commander Gabriel quickly strategizes. "Then you must hurry, my friend! Resistance is being met in every tunnel. I cannot guarantee your safety, but yes, you must hurry. I will radio for a truck to be ready." Boarding the jeep, they speed away. Glancing back, Jacob spies aviators swarming the B-17. He smugly smiles.

A sudden dust storm threatens as Zac, Nick, Jacob, and their soldier escort arrive.

Jacob cautions Zac and Nick, "Stay behind the soldiers! In the tunnels, they tend to target anyone not in an Israeli uniform!"

Nick turns to Zac. "Stay behind me!"

"No problem." Zac is happy to comply.

As Zac turns towards the tunnel, a troubled Jacob grabs his arm. "Your father... Zac, I'm sorry. He ran back to retrieve his notes." Jacob laments, "I should've told you sooner. There was a flash, then an explosion. We looked, but—"

Zac suddenly sprints. Ignoring commands to stop, he disappears into the tunnel. The others hurry to catch up.

Muscles tense as they enter the tunnel. Distant, sporadic explosions shake dirt from the ceiling. The three soldiers abruptly hold their position as one soldier takes the lead and motions them forward. Raising theirs guns, they cautiously advance, sweeping their guns from side to side. Nick and Jacob stay close behind. They soon arrive at their destination, only to find Zac standing in awe before the Ark.

"We're in time!" Jacob takes over. "Don't touch the Ark!" Jacob turns to the demolition soldier and points. "There, we're going to mark and seal this location!"

Explosions are getting closer as sandbags are carefully placed around the Ark for protection.

Zac sees blood splatters on the Ark. "Dad?"

"That's not your father's blood," Jacob assures.

"But I thought you said no blood ever touched the Ark?"

An anxious Jacob reminds Zac, "Beck will be here, make no mistake, there's no time to waste!"

Zac scans the area. "Where could he be? Did you look—"

"I'm sorry." Jacob interrupts, "We searched, heaven knows, but found nothing!"

Nick hurries towards Zac but stops, awed by the Ark. "Zac. C'mon, let's... Holy Moses."

Zac yells to Jacob, "If you can't touch it, how'd you get a blood sample? I'm open to—" A deafening explosion interrupts.

As loosened debris falls, a jostled Jacob hollers back, "Not now! We can open it later!"

Zac cautions. "Trust me, that's a bad idea." Zac's hand slowly reaches out, daring to touch the Ark. Nick and Jacob are quick to pull Zac towards the exit. He protests. "Hey, I was only... Wait, what if...?" A soldier puts the last sandbag in place, then lights an exceptionally long fuse.

Zac leads the way, hustling as they run out in single file. They 'round a blind corner just as Beck and his henchmen race in the opposite direction, towards the Ark, in single file and only inches away. Zac skids to a stop as the others stumble one into the other. Nick and Zac look at each other.

"Was that—?" Nick asks.

Zac's hand shoots up. "This is not happening." He takes a deep breath before racing back. The others hurry to catch up. As they enter the chamber, a firefight erupts. One Israeli soldier falls, wounded.

A henchman eagerly lights a stick of dynamite, but Zac quickly takes aim and shoots it out of his hand. All helplessly watch it rolls under the Ark. When the henchman stoops to retrieve the dynamite, he accidently touches the Ark and glows brightly before disappearing.

Zac quickly reacts. Dodging bullets, he rushes to grab the dynamite. Pulling the fuse, he stands and smiles. Quickly taking aim, Beck shoots, striking Zac just below his heart. Nick and Jacob stare in horror.

"*Zac!*" Nick yells.

Zac looks down at his wound in disbelief. He grabs his side and stumbles, touching the Ark. Zac vanishes in a flash of light.

(April 3, 33 A.D.) Darkness covers the land as the ground endlessly trembles. Looking upwards, Zac is mystified by a universe of lackluster stars. His gaze is drawn to the presence of the Taurus constellation. As he tries to focus, Zac is jostled by ghostly images rushing chaotically in all directions. He soon realizes that the images are frightened people.

Suddenly, a distant, familiar voice rings out, "Zac? Son!" It's his father! Elated, Zac turns and sees his father's silhouette atop a small mound.

Zac shouts as he attempts to maneuver through the frantic masses, "Dad, stay there!" He reaches the top of the mound and quickly looks about. Clutching his wound, Zac hears a moan and turns to see the henchman hanging on a cross. Shocked and puzzled, he stumbles back and bumps into another, on a cross, between two others. Looking up, Zac scans a sign above the man and quickly realizes that this is indeed, Jesus Christ! Zac's upward gaze is drawn beyond Christ to the star known as Aldebaran. He remembers that, in Hebrew, it represented 'aleph', or God. Looking down, he is suddenly transfixed at the 't' shape of the Cross. It hits him, "Of course, the Cross represents 't', symbolizing 'tav', which would translate as 'on the cross'.

Overwhelmed at the scope of this revelation, Zac murmurs, "aleph and tav....God on the cross!" Shaken to his core, Zac realizes that he is witness to Jesus being proclaimed by YHVH as God!

Turning, Zac is stunned, overwhelmed at the sight of Christ lifting His tortured body by the nails. Momentarily suspended,

Christ gazes upwards before summoning a mighty and victorious SHOUT, causing all to tremble! From his vantage, Zac spies the veil of the Temple as it is rent from top to bottom. The earth rumbles and violently shakes. Zac then stares in disbelief as he watches the blood moon, in retrograde, give way to the returning sun.

Zac cannot believe that all of this has been kept from the world. He then recalls that the chief priests were frantic about what Pilate had written and placed above the cross. He flinches when a drop of the Christ's blood falls on his face.

A Roman Centurion climbs the knoll, muttering something in an old German dialect. He pushes Zac aside and examines Christ on the Cross. Zac suddenly finds himself in a position to read the sign Pilate has placed above the Cross.

"Son!"

Momentarily startled, Zac focuses as he visually backtracks to where he was earlier standing, and sees his father. Waving, Zac shouts, "Dad, don't move!"

The centurion thrusts his spear into Christ's side. Zac recoils in pain, then stares in amazement as his wound is cauterized. A sharp tremor knocks him to one knee as the ground below the cross is rent. Fixated on Christ, Zac watches as water mixed with blood pour from Christ's side and down a crack suddenly enlarged by the tremor.

In a flash, he finds himself in a chamber below the cross. Looking up, towards a crack in the ceiling, he sees blood emerge and pool before falling onto the Ark. Another jolt knocks Zac forward, but he is promptly caught by two angelic figures. Both suddenly appear surprised. Looking towards the Ark, Zac and the two figures watch as the Ark slowly begins to vanish. The two stunned cherubim release Zac who lands with a thud that propels him back to the firefight.

As he staggers, the soldiers lay suppressive fire, while Nick and Jacob rush to pull Zac to safety. A lone henchman keeps all pinned with a machinegun as Beck and the others carry the Ark away. Zac points to a stalactite hanging above the henchman and all fire, bringing it down on the henchman.

"The Ark!" Zac exclaims.

A soldier sees the shorter, burning fuse and shouts, "Double time!"

"This is going to be close," Nick quickly asserts.

All rush out as the explosion's billowing dust and debris overtakes them. They emerge to Israeli soldiers firing at an escaping truck.

"There they go?" Zac points.

"Hey, that's our truck!" Nick yells.

Zac's attention is drawn to merchants in the distance, arguing next to an idling flatbed ice cream truck. He smirks.

Zac leaps into the truck. Grinding gears, he halts any pursuit by spinning the tires and kicking up his own dust storm. Amid shouts and flailing gestures, he speeds away. He stops just long enough to pick up Jacob. Nick and a soldier leap onto the back. While Zac searches for a gear, the wounded soldier tosses his rifle to Nick. All hang on as Zac hits the gas.

As the truck careens through Jerusalem, a harried Jacob feels compelled to ask, "Zac, are you alright?"

"Thought so." Zac is enigmatic.

As they pass the airport exit, Jacob exclaims, "The airport! I thought... Where are we going?"

Zac murmurs, "I've got a bad feeling about this."

Climbing a hill, Zac stops and looks westward to see the truck in the distance, heading towards the sea. A fiercely determined Zac gives chase.

They slow as they enter a fishing village. Attempting to push through the busy street, Zac hits the horn but there is no sound. He sees a dangling rope to his left. Thinking it must be the horn, he pulls it. The worn rope breaks, but not before starting the ice cream truck's whimsical bell ringing. The incessant chime draws children from every direction. Making their way towards the beach, they spy a small boat, just offshore, loading the Ark onto a U-boat.

"There they are!" Jacob exclaims.

Punching the gas, Zac speeds onto the beach.

The soldier's helmet flies off. Nick can't believe his eyes. "Yahtzee!" The soldier is female and beautiful.

"Nazis!" Zac grumbles.

Beck and his henchmen frantically level a barrage of gunfire. Zac and Jacob duck as, over the truck cab, Nick, and the soldier return fire. Nick quickly dispatches two with two shots, impressing the soldier.

Fearing the volley of bullets, Beck hurries down the hatch, abandoning the last henchman. The U-boat begins moving back, submerging stern first. The churning the waters trap and drown the terrified henchman.

Zac spots something rushing towards them just below the water's surface. The U-boat has fired a torpedo. It shoots out of the water and onto the beach. Skimming across the sand, it stops with a thump, under the ice cream truck. Taking the deadly cue, all leap and run towards the nearest dune. Tense moments later, the blast rips the truck apart. The children arrive to a shower of raining ice cream bars.

"What happened?" Nick is surprised that they're all still alive.

"Must've been set for distance." Zac explains. "We were too close." Zac and Nick shade themselves from the sun as the children suddenly begin to cry and hold their heads. Nick picks up and eats an ice cream cone as Zac comments, "In this heat, instant brain freeze."

"Augh!" Nick suddenly grabs his head.

Zac can't resist. "Bring any merit badges?"

CHAPTER 9

A T A NEARBY infirmary, bruises and flesh wounds are tended to. A doctor sees the bloodstained bullet hole in Zac's shirt. He approaches but Zac takes a cavalier attitude, "No, I'm fine, really."

The doctor points to the examining table and is insistent, "I'll do the diagnosing, thank you."

Zac halfheartedly resists as the doctor becomes captivated by the slanted, cauterized scar. "Most interesting... Bullet must've tumbled as it hit, more like a knife or lance wound. Something familiar..."

"Fascinating!" Overhearing the doctor, Jacob approaches. "Zac, you vanished, where were you?"

Aware of the surrounding medical staff, Zac searches for words, "I saw them... Him!" Zac looks at Jacob and struggles with what he saw. "The blood...I was there... And dad was there, too!"

"I don't believe it!" Jacob is both relieved and profoundly amazed.

Another doctor approaches. Intrigued, he quickly addresses Jacob, "Are you suggesting this wound is a psychosomatic reaction?"

Jacob reacts, "Heaven's no! I mean, he was shot, he touched the Ark and vanished. What he saw... Zac, what did you see?"

A third doctor now eagerly gazes at the wound, then questions Jacob, "Are you suggesting psychogenic purpura?"

Puzzled, Jacob hesitates. "Well... I don't know—"

"Wait, what? I know! No, oh, no!" Zac protests.

The second doctor quickly addresses Zac, "Are you subject to periodical apparitions?"

Zac raises a cautionary finger and snaps back, "Don't even think—"

"Is he your patient?" The first doctor interrupts as he anxiously addresses Jacob.

Zac becomes belligerent. "Hey. I am not... Now just a minute!"

The second doctor, lost to his own imaginings, quickly turns his head, and sniffs the air. "The odor of sanctity... Stigmata!"

Stunned by the comment, Zac hops off the table and quickly buttons his shirt. "Alright, enough. I am not...this is not a Stigmata wound. I was shot... Okay?" Glancing out the window, he gestures to the jasmine growing outside as he tucks his shirt. "I know... Jasmine, the scent of the Stigmata. I know, but it's coming from outside, *not-my-side!*"

A frantic and troubled field commander enters. "Gentlemen, is everyone alright? The Ark... Is it true?"

"We'll get it back." Zac fails to be reassuring.

"Ah! You've lost the Ark?" Commander Gabriel raises his arms in frustration.

Nick tries his hand at reassurance. "Don't worry, we'll get it back, I promise."

Gabriel laments, "For centuries the Ark has preserved our very existence. Now, its power, in the hands of our enemies."

Jacob appears hesitant as he looks at Zac and Nick but remains encouraging. "I assure you; we will find it."

Commander Gabriel becomes hopeful but insistent, "Pray, my friend, and then pray again because you cannot fail."

Nick slides the action on his shotgun. "Don't worry. Look, we've got the only two men qualified to find the Ark." Zac and Jacob look at each other. Nick can't resist. "Of course, they're the only two to lose an Ark." Jacob and Zac glare at Nick who tries to ease the tension. "But I'm sure—"

"Look, we'll find the Ark." Zac interrupts.

"How?" The Commander challenges Zac.

Zac fumbles for an answer, "We...find the U-boat."

"Where?" Gabriel tests Zac further.

"In... Under..." Zac tries but loses his patients. "Now look—"

"You know," Nick quickly intercedes, "we should be leaving."

"Good idea." Jacob chimes in.

Commander Gabriel advises, "I'm afraid you'll have to wait, my friend. I've cleared you for the continued use of the B-17G, but it will not be ready until morning. I suggest you all get some rest."

Zac agrees. "Better idea, and some food."

Nick looks at Zac. "Sure, how fast can a U-boat go?"

The commander continues, "Yes, meanwhile, I will discuss this with intelligence. I hope you don't mind sharing a room."

All of them are assigned to barracks no. 36. As they approach the barracks, a wind whips up and rattles a loose number. It swings down and barracks 39 suddenly reads 36. Zac and Nick eagerly carry sandwiches and bottles of sodas.

Zac enters first and quickly points to a small table on his right. "Is that an alarm clock?"

Nick tosses it out the window. Before eating, Zac and Nick cannot resist stretching out on their assigned beds.

"I'm going with the commander," Jacob states. He is not trusting of Zac or Nick and adds, "And for heaven's sake, be here when I get back."

Zac's eyes are closed as he responds, "Fine, sure, let us know..."

Nick too, is fading fast. "Great, we'll be waiting..." Zac and Nick fall fast asleep.

CHAPTER 10

J ACOB RUSHES INTO the moonlit room and jostles Zac and Nick awake. Instinctively, both sit up and point their guns at Jacob.

"Hurry, we have an appointment." An anxious Jacob suddenly becomes suspicious. "Wait, I smell perfume!" Fearing indiscretions, Jacob becomes accusatory. "I don't believe it! Of all the times to—" Zac flips a light switch, stopping Jacob's rant. A rousing, shuffling noise freezes Zac, Nick, and Jacob. All slowly turn their heads and attention to a bevy of sleepy heads now gazing their way.

The barracks erupt into shouts and screams from female soldiers, mostly in issued nightwear. Our trio is at a loss for words as a flurry of shoes and women's apparel rain down on them.

"Whoa! We can explain!" Nick shouts.

"We can?" Zac quickly ducks. "Hey, watch it!"

Jacob is quick to clean his glasses. He puts them on and smiles, "Oh, my! May I—" Jacob is swiftly hit with a barrage of pillows.

Nick gets an idea. "A-TEN-SHUN!" The soldiers snap to attention.

Nick stands, grinning from ear to ear. Before he can say anything, Zac grabs him by the collar and yanks him away as they make a hasty retreat. Outside, a truck is waiting.

Speeding through Jerusalem, they are driven to the Desert Sands, an afterhours nightclub, rich in clandestine meetings and where secret friends of Israel go to unwind.

As they approach, Nick notes a somewhat vague similarity to a place back home. "Hey, Desert Sands, reminds me of a place in Vegas."

Zac just shakes his head.

Nick continues, "You know, the gunnery school near Vegas?" He reminisces, "The crowds that gathered during testing. Picnicking, just waiting for that mushroom cloud. Ever see one of those things?"

"No thanks." Zac answers as he sizes-up their surroundings.

Jacob knocks on the door.

"What, no secret knock?" Nick wisecracks.

Nick's quip is countered by Zac who offers some savvy wisdom, "Nothing draws attention like a secret knock."

An uneasy Nick puts his hand on his gun as he looks around. "Why does it feel like we're being watched?"

"Because we are." Zac has spied two figures crouched on the roof.

Jacob is quick to add, "Get that hand down! Yes, two snipers at our six high. This place is well protected, quite secure."

The door opens just as the band begins to play and a familiar female, wearing a black dress, and minus her helmet, begins singing. She smiles and gestures towards Nick with a nod and a wink. Nick finds himself smitten. In an aimless stride, he returns an awkward smile, before bumping into a beam. Unhurt, except for his ego, he catches up with the others. They approach a table where a scruffy, mustachioed individual nervously lights up before an already overflowing ashtray. He adjusts his eyepatch as Zac and Nick pull up chairs.

Jacob speaks up, "You must be—"

"No names, please." Abrupt and insistent, the contact glances up with his good eye.

The barmaid brings a round of drinks. "Complements of the Sultan."

Zac, Nick, and Jacob spy a backlit figure gesturing a toast as he sits in what is apparently a privileged guest area. All of them return the gesture.

The overture has momentarily lifted the contact's spirits. He raises his glass high and smiles. "Now there is a good friend of the Israeli people. But to the point, Jacob tells me you're searching for a submarine, a U-boat." The contact leans in, drawing the others in as well. "To hunt this U-boat, you must believe the myths are true, as the Nazis do."

"There are a lot of myths." Zac makes his skepticism known.

The contact smiles before challenging Zac, "How many would you say require the use of U-boats?" All stare at each other, then back at the contact who continues, "Towards the end, U-boats were seen continuously moving up and down rivers. Why? Escape?"

Zac comes to a fearful realization and takes a deep breath. "Let's cut to the chase, we're looking for a Redoubt. And please, tell me I'm wrong."

"A what?" Nick is confused.

The contact explains, "A Redoubt, a fortress designed for a last stand. In this case, we believe, a last course of action to be implemented at some future date."

"For the Nazis, it never happened." Zac speaks with an uneasy confidence.

The contact puts out his cigarette. "Not yet."

"Don't!" Zac glances about as he grumbles, "That's how rumors get started."

Jacob draws on an obvious conclusion, "But subs in the rivers, rivers flow from mountains, a mountain fortress, makes sense."

"Too easy to find." Zac disagrees. The barmaid's tray of multi-sized drinks inspires Zac. "A castle!"

The contact nods. "That is our belief. Much can be hidden in a castle."

Jacob is bewildered. "But there are dozens of castles along dozens of rivers. We haven't the time."

Zac surmises, "I'm thinking not much would need to be hidden. I mean, the war created an unbeatable allied war machine. No, what they'd need were post-war plans involving espionage or maybe sabotage but on a grand scale, and a timetable. U-boats could be useful."

Nick raises a sobering prospect, "Wouldn't they still need outsiders to carry out such elaborate plans?"

Zac looks around the room. "Sympathizers? There were plenty before the war. Nazis cultivated their eugenic ideology with the help of elitists."

Jacob chimes on, "I say, in the states, Sanger popularized this ideology... Made it her life's work!" He laments a bitter fact. "Hard to believe we still pander to the twisted science of eugenics."

Zac sees Jacob's zealousness going a little off topic, and adds, "Hitler's actions showed the world what eugenics' true colors were all about."

The contact nods. "Unsettled a lot of Germans."

"Too few, too late," Nick adds.

"Indeed!" Jacob is quick to agree.

"After the war, the mad rush for Nazi technology pretty much gave everyone amnesia." Zac's bitterness is obvious.

"And re-invented the business of spying. Everybody went nuts, grabbing all they could."

"Gentlemen." Their contact attempts to interjects, but to no avail.

"What ever happened to sharing?" Nick manages a philosophical sarcasm.

Jacob ponders. "Every square mile must've been gone through. Hard to believe anything would've been missed."

A suspicious Zac looks at the contact. "Exactly what are we here for?"

"Yes." The contact finishes lighting another cigarette. "Well, there is this one castle, officially off limits, something about being haunted. Interested?"

A contemptuous Zac remarks, "Superstitious mumbo jumbo."

"So, you'll go? Perfect."

Nick leans back. "I might know this castle. As a matter of fact, when we—"

"You? You were with intelligence?" A startled Zac chides Nick.

Nick retaliates, "You're not the only one that can read a map. Why are you here, anyway?"

A defiant Zac gets in Nick's face. "Because I make the maps you read."

Nick snarls back, "Aren't you a guest of the Professor?"

Jacob takes a verbal jab at Nick, "Guest? Why, Zac's skills are beyond reproach!" Guest, my—"

"Jacob!" Zac quickly interrupts, "Thanks."

The contact tries to hide his amusement at the bickering. "Gentlemen...are you through?"

Both Nick and Zac, still somewhat riled, shift uneasily in their seats.

Jacob addresses the contact while visually admonishing Zac and Nick, "We apologize, please continue."

While sharply tapping his finger on the table, the contact proceeds but with an emphatic cadence to his delivery, "You must focus, you must believe that Hitler's Redoubt is in existence and that plans for a counterattack may be imminent!"

"C'mon, it's been eleven years." Zac resists the notion. "You don't really think...?"

"Dr. Gomes, when such stories are validated by U-boats and such men as this Mr. Beck."

"Precisely." Jacob quickly agrees.

The contact continues, "For now, believe the myths."

"Zac, still skeptical after all you've been through?" Nick chides.

"I understand they have the Ark. Pray it's not too late. It may be suicide to continue." The contact nervously lights yet another cigarette as he glances at Nick before addressing all, "Do you know what it means to sacrifice... even another?" Zac shifts in his chair as he suspects that last question was intended for Nick.

Jacob becomes anxious. "Where is this castle?"

"Germany." Nick states matter-of-factly.

Zac folds his hands behind his head and delivers a slow, drawn-out sarcasm, "Why am I not surprised? I mean, of course, that's great Nick, you're just one surprise after another.

"Excuse me!" Jacob calls loudly for the barmaid. "Please, drinks all around."

Nearby, a tired aviator perks up and turns towards Jacob. "Drinks all around! Americans! B-17!"

"They found me, Great Saint Arnold!" Jacob laments.

Nick looks inquisitively at a puzzled Zac who responds, "Patron Saint of brewers." Zac quickly turns to Jacob. "Wait, you promised them free drinks?"

Jacob sits, resigned to his fate. "I was caught up in the moment. Really, how much can they drink?"

Zac is all too eager to explain, "Well, desert pilots, fighting in hot, metal cockpits, in zero humidity, 100 plus heat, all day, every day."

"Oh, my." Jacob quietly laments.

The door suddenly opens to a dozen boisterous aviators who quickly join in the festivities as another round comes, compliments of the Sultan.

Zac and the others quickly down their drinks and rise to leave. They see the Sultan rises and strolls towards the band; his face still hidden in the shadows.

Jacob's wallet empties.

Nick has been admiring the female soldier turned singer when she suddenly gestures towards the mystery guest and gracefully announces, "It looks like the Sultan's going to honor us with a song."

Applause erupts as Zac quietly speaks his mind, "Everybody's a singer."

As they approach the door to leave, the armed bouncer quickly raises a hand. Zac and Nick are startled by the sound of two muffled shots. Instinctively, they reach for their guns, but the bouncer's stern glance is warning enough. Two hard thumps on the other side of the door are heard. When the bouncer opens the door, two bodies fall halfway in.

From outside, soldiers emerge from the shadows as the wind whips back shirts on the bodies, revealing weapons. The bodies are swiftly dragged away. Zac and Nick look at the bouncer who is running a finger down his clipboard.

With a heavy accent, he gruffly states, "Not on list."

Jacob takes the front seat as Zac and Nick climb in the back. Seeing that dawn is fast approaching, their driver hits the gas.

A curious Nick asks, "So what country's this Sultan from?"

Jacob laughs. "Country? It's just a term of endearment. He's not a real Sultan. All this time neither of you knew?"

Bewildered, Zac and Nick look at each other. Jacob is enjoying the look on their faces. "He's known in the States as the Sultan of Swoon."

Zac and Nick look at each other and together exclaim, "SINATRA!"

Their truck careens as Zac demands, "Turn this truck around!"

Nick joins Zac in protest. "You could've told us."

Zac tries talking tough, "Jacob, I'm serious! Driver... excuse me... Driver?"

An anxious Nick tries a halfhearted threat on Jacob, "You're riding in the tail."

"Sinatra... I'm getting dizzy." Zac feigns illness.

Nick follows suit. "I'm going to be sick."

Jacob, still enjoying Zac and Nick's childish lament, admonishes both with a reminder, "Sorry but it's going to be light soon, and we don't want to be sitting ducks again, now do we?"

While glaring at Jacob, Nick asks Zac, "Exactly how long can it take to find a body in the desert...weeks?"

Gazing at Jacob, Zac responds with a wry smirk, "Centuries."

The morning sun glistens off the B-17 as it quickly soars. Jacob struggles with the cramped, tail gunners' quarters when a Sinatra song loudly crackles through his headphones, courtesy of a vengeful Nick. Jacob can't help but smiles.

CHAPTER 11

D RIVING THROUGH A small village, traffic is stopped by a procession, led by the local Rabbi.

Zac takes the opportunity to continue his dirge-like complaint, "A simple autograph, I mean..."

"I thought he looked a little familiar." Nick adds.

Zac teases. "After all those toasts, I bet everybody looked a little familiar."

"Gentlemen, it just struck me." Jacob attempts to chime in.

"Did you hear anything?" Nick is still upset.

Just then, a flock of geese can be heard flying overhead.

Zac plays along. "Must be the geese?" As if on cue, goose droppings strike Zac's hat. His eyes widen in disbelief.

"You see! Respect your elders!" Jacob can't resist the opportunity,

As Zac cleans his hat, people from the procession hurry towards their truck. All clutch photos of missing loved ones. An elderly couple approach and thrust a photo at Zac. He nods and offers a nervous smile as he reluctantly accepts the tattered photograph, that is, until he looks at it. "She's beautiful."

The father sharply taps his cane on the cobblestone, demanding attention. In his desperation and with a heavy accent he pleads, "Please, she is Sarah, our daughter!"

The mother clasps Zac's hand holding the picture. "She is a doctor. We know she was taken." Her hand wavers as she stumbles towards Zac. Being pushed by the crowd, she, in turn, pushes the picture against him. "Take it, please, take it, and God bless."

Others rush in, extending photos, crowding out the couple in the process.

A sympathizing Nick offers a sad fact, "After the war, thousands were unaccounted for."

Jacob suggests, "Isn't that just a tragedy of war? I mean, people disappear."

Nick agrees, "Right, wouldn't have meant much if it weren't for all the missing U-boats. We figured if we could track just one U-boat, we'll find the rest."

"And just who exactly are we?" Once again, Zac's curiosity about Nick are stirred.

Nick quickly changes the subject. "Look, there's the castle! Ten minutes, tops." Nick guns the engine and begins the climb towards the foreboding, silhouetted castle.

At the castle, two nervous soldiers almost cheer as our trio approaches. A smiling Nick hops out to help a no-nonsense, but slightly superstitious sergeant pull a crate from their small truck.

Zac gazes at the castle. "Got a funny feeling about this place."

"Yes, I— Now what are those for?" Jacob's response is interrupted by an unexpected sight.

Nick and the sergeant pull machine guns from the crate as Nick explains, "Look, Jacob, believe it or not, soldiers are still being found, still at their post, unaware that the war is over?" He slaps a magazine into his Thompson. "And I don't like surprises?"

"Really?" Zac resists the notion.

Nick teases, "Aren't you the cautious one?"

The private grabs a weapon but the sergeant takes hold of it. "Hold on, you stay out here with the truck." The sergeant returns the gun and reaches for a grappling hook and launcher.

The young private protests, "Hey, you know I can't drive."

"That's why I chose you," the sergeant explains. "Rich boys being chauffeured about don't learn much about driving, do they?" The sergeant adjusts his equipment.

"Nothing wrong with being rich." The private gets defensive.

"Yeah, yeah, I know." The sergeant nods and then confides, "Look, castles give me the creeps and I didn't want somebody getting the heebie-jeebies and taking off on us. Just stay sharp, and don't break anything. Got it?"

"Yes, sir."

The private suddenly has an idea. He strolls over and taps Zac on the shoulder. "Sir, could I trouble you to show me how—"

Quickly raising a hand, a busy Zac stops the private mid-sentence. He glances at the truck. "I heard. Sorry kid, can't help you."

The private implores Zac, "Please sir, just a gear or two?" An impatient Zac looks again at the truck then at the private.

Slapping a hand on the private's shoulder, Zac leans in and with a stern finger waving, rushes an explanation, "Look, 1st, clutch in—",

"You mean, 1st gear is—"

"Don't interrupt." Zac quickly silences the private.

"No, sir." The private responds apologetically.

Zac continues, "2nd, move stick left, then all the way forward." The private is intrigued. Satisfied with himself and his instructions, Zac finishes, "3rd, release the clutch." Zac becomes distracted when Nick hands him a torch.

The private quietly recites Zac's lesson, "So, 1st - clutch in, 2nd - stick left, then forward, 3rd - release the clutch." The private asks a busy Zac one more question, "Excuse me, is there a 4th?"

A busy Zac tosses a response, "What? Look kid, just pull the stick back for the next gear." The young private smiles, now beaming with confidence. Nick hands Jacob a torch then motions everyone towards the castle entrance.

Crossing the drawbridge, they slowly walk down a long, damp corridor. Their raised torches seem to grow dimmer with every step, as if the darkness were consuming them. Having taken the lead, Zac stops and turns. The flickering glow of his torch on their faces reveals a collective uneasiness. Turning back, he points his torch away and towards the ground and proceeds with caution. With his next step, he freezes as the castle floor ends. Raising their torches, they gaze at an immense, seemingly hollowed-out castle tower, maybe 60 feet in diameter. Peering over the ledge, Zac stares into utter darkness.

"Hand me that extra torch."

Nick obliges. When Zac tosses it over the edge, all slowly lean forward, watching and listening, but it disappears without a sound.

"Bottomless." Nick is shaken and backs up.

"I've never seen one of these." Zac's curiosity is aroused.

"There just a legend." Jacob scoffs.

"What is it?" The sergeant's nervousness is apparent.

"A gateway." Nick quietly speaks.

Zac gazes down the abyss as he states matter-of-factly, "To hell, or so they say."

Nerves get the best of the sergeant as he quickly turns, bidding farewell as he walks, "Check, please! I'm outta here! Adios muchachos! Sayonara!"

In his haste, the sergeant unwittingly steps on a pressure plate. The massive drawbridge springs upwards but is jarred to a stop halfway by rusted chains anchoring it to the ground. Startled, all of them look at each other before making a mad dash. The rotted chain posts fail. Ripped from their mooring, they send the massive drawbridge slamming shut.

The sergeant's nerves get the best of him. "*Nick*...you said this'd be a piece of cake, in and out, ten minutes, tops... *Sir!*"

All the while, Zac is surveying two doors, one on either side of the corridor.

Nick raises a hand, silencing the sergeant's tirade. He has also noticed the doors and pulls out a coin. He flips it and calls, "Heads left, tails right."

Zac snatches the coin midair. "I've got a hunch."

"A hunch?" Nick queries.

Jacob defends Zac. "I say, an educated 'hunch' is far better than some random—"

"Hold on there, Jake," the sergeant interrupts. As the sergeant attempts to explain, an annoyed Jacob looks at Zac and sarcastically mimes the word 'Jake' with his mouth. "It's a well-known fact that, throughout history, 50/50 has always had better success."

Nick chimes in, "Always worked for me."

"We have three choices?" Zac throws a curve.

The sergeant fumbles for a response, "Oh... Well, in that case... Uh—"

"Great Saint Cayetano!" Jacob is flabbergasted.

"Gambling?" Nick quizzes Zac.

Zac nods.

Suddenly, the castle shakes violently.

Nick yells, "*Earthquake!*" All of them are knocked off balance. Zac, already standing by the edge, falls off.

"*Zac!*" Nick reaches out, but too late.

The shaking stops and all rush to the edge just as Zac pops his head and shoulders up from a ledge he's landed on. "Just as I thought, follow me."

Jacob boasts, "What'd I tell you?"

All jump down and begin navigating the protruding wooden steps as they spiral up and around the massive stone tower. Unseen, every step they've passed has slowly retracted into the wall. Ahead of all, Zac barely stops in time as the steps abruptly end. An inattentive Nick bumps into Zac, causing Zac's boot to slip on a loose fragment. It falls, disappearing into the darkness. To their surprise, it strikes what sounds like an enormous, metal drum.

Nick winces at the noise and begins to complain, "Whose side you on...? Hey!"

"Yeah, that wasn't there a minute ago." Zac finishes Nick's thought.

Jacob, being last, sees the steps retracting. "Oh, my. I say... Excuse me."

"I'm surprised we haven't come across anymore booby traps." The sergeant comments.

"What, one wasn't enough?" Nick's remark suddenly reminds him of Zac's earlier comment. "Besides, nothing draws attention like a booby trap."

Nick's teaser doesn't escape Zac's attention as he deadpans Nick who smiles broadly.

"*I say!*" Jacob shouts his concern. "We seem to be losing our ability to retreat!" All turn and extend their torches for a better look.

"There's your booby trap." Nick gets sarcastic. "Happy?"

"Now what?" A panicked sergeant exclaims.

Zac shouts, "Nobody move!"

Too late, Jacob has put one foot on the next step and triggered his step's retraction. Jacob slips as the sergeant grabs and pulls him onto his step.

"Thank you."

The step supporting the sergeant and Jacob slowly begins to retract as both hurry onto Nick's creaking and now overloaded step.

"Uh, Zac." Nick desperately tries to maintain his balance.

"Hang on, I'm thinking!" Zac frantically searches the area for a way out. Looking down, he spots a doorway 30 feet away and well below their position. He spots what appear to be wooden steps, recessed into the wall. Visually backtracking, he follows them to a protruding wooden beam attached below and perpendicular to the step he is on.

Nicks step suddenly cracks.

"*I say again... ZAC!*" Nick shouts as he and the others to urgently search for a handhold on the wall.

Zac hazards a hunch. "This better work."

He steps off.

"*NO!*" Nick yells as all helplessly watch Zac seemingly step into the darkness.

Zac drops his foot onto the beam. As it moves downward, he watches the recessed wooden steps slowly emerge. The last step protrudes above the beam Zac is on. Raising a foot onto the new step causes the beam to spring upwards and lock under his step, cleverly securing the others in place. Zac darts down the steps while the others scurry onto the newly protruding planks. Zac reaches the door and handily deciphers its symbols. He pushes one, then another, and the door swings inward.

The sergeant is impressed. "Man, you're full of tricks."

"Tricks?" Jacob protests.

"What, no Patron Saint?" Nick jokes.

Zac looks away and nonchalantly answers as he enters the room. "Saint Bosco, magicians."

Nick eagerly enters after Zac and is amazed. "Will ya look at this?" Jacob and the sergeant scurry in, happy to be on solid footing and off those steps.

Inside they discover documents, star charts and endless Nazi paraphernalia. A single stained-glass window illuminates the room. Hanging overhead are detailed wooden models of what appear to be rocket prototypes. They sit at a table under a full-size flying wing prototype and share the task of shuffling through a plethora of artifacts.

Nick glances at Zac and pays him an off-handed compliment, "We never would've found this room."

"Hey, what's with this sword?" The sergeant makes an intriguing discovery as all soon realize the room is devoid of metal and that everything is made of wood.

Nick taps the tip of a pendulum placed over a map. "Here's some metal."

Zac suddenly thinks aloud, "Now why would they want a demagnetized room?"

Jacob is preoccupied with journals from an abandoned satchel. "It seems the Nazis were desperate to get into space."

"According to this, they may have made it." Zac is intrigued by a map of the stars.

Nick falls back onto a chair in disbelief. "Tell me you're kidding."

Jacob is quick to add his findings. "Yes, these notes state that they were in constant telepathic communication with beings from the Aldebaran star system. Apparently, these beings nurtured the idea of an Aryan race whose rightful place was ruling the world."

"There's your mumbo jumbo," Nick remarks.

Jacob turns the page. "Nick, that coin of yours, it's here, look!"

Walking towards Jacob, Nick retrieve the coin and casually flips it towards him. Zac again snatches it midair.

After studying it, he asks, "Where'd you get this?"

Nick hesitates, then shares a brief encounter, "An S.S. Colonel got the drop on me." Nick becomes animated as he retells his story, "I can still remember his quaint, little smile as he cheerfully sauntered towards me, keeping aim as he approached. Then he whips out that coin. Heads, he shoots, tails..." Nick smiles. "He got a little too close."

Zac smirks as he flips the coin back to Nick, "It's a 200-year-old coin called the Bull's Eye. Turning back, he taps his finger on the star chart. "The Aldebaran System is in the eye of the Taurus constellation, the bull's eye, as it's called." Zac pauses, suddenly recalling his 'journey' to the crucifixion. He turns. "Jacob, I saw it, all of it, Taurus, Aldebaran...and a blood moon...all at the Crucifixion."

Nick comments, "So you think there's a connection?"

"Ah!" Jacob is seemingly inspired.

The room grows quiet as all eyes become fixed on Jacob. The sun is shining brightly through the stained-glass window, Its warmth draws his gaze.

"So, the story holds true... That the sun was darkened, revealing a universe of stars that had miraculously lost their luster...and a blood moon, prematurely risen. Zac, Isaiah 13:13 states that *"-the earth shall be moved out of her place-"*, and Amos 8:9, *"-I will cause the sun to go down at noon-"*. Pilate wrote of the pervasive tremors, lasting through the three hours of darkness. I believe he also made mention of a blood moon."

He suddenly becomes animated. "Of course, the sun went down! Zac...the two pagan philosophers, Dionysius and Appollophanes, in Egypt at the time of the Crucifixion! Both claimed to have watched the moon rise and align itself with the sun's vacated position! *That would explain Phlegon's claim of the strangest of solar eclipse since, during a full moon, such an eclipse is impossible!"*

Zac can't believe what he's hearing. "You're saying that the earth did a quick one-eighty and then, in recovery, returned...3 hours later?"

Jacob ponders, "And *that* explains the continuous tremors!"

Zac adjusts his posture as he tempers a retort, "Hold on! You're saying that God rolled the earth, in preparation, in anticipation of Christ's death...? Why...? And is that even possible?"

Jacob retorts, "Well, Hapgood, and Einstein might have something to say about it. The theory goes, I believe, that if, say, an asteroid or meteor of sufficient mass were to strike the earth at just the right angle and speed, it could cause a global shift. It would bring about precisely the events witnessed at the Crucifixion!"

"Guys...you lost me."

Ignoring Nick, Zac queries, "That strike would have to occur during a full moon."

Jacob is impressed. "Yes, the sun and moon would have to be in opposition, so the theory states. It's the only way the earth could recover from such an event." He glances at Nick, "Indeed, the earth is always in flux, thanks to our vast oceans." Jacob paces. "The earth's accelerated rotation would cause the sun to appear to set, as the blood moon would appear to rise from below the horizon." Jacob recounts, "'*After 3 hours, the moon, in retrograde, gave way to the sun as it returned.*' Yes...again, as reported by Dionysius and Appollophanes!"

"But... What are the odds?"

"Zac, my boy, there is a particular, suspect group of celestial bodies that intersect earth's orbit... Who's to say...?" Jacob pauses and queries, "What else did you see?"

Zac ponders, "I saw the blood, His blood fall on the Ark."

Jacob nods, quietly reflecting, "Temple sacrifices were always performed in the dark, for a period of 3 hours." He glances about the room. "You do know that miracles often involve the manipulation of physical laws as God wills?"

All gesture a collective, though unconvincing affirmation.

In a bit of a huff, Jacob punctuates, *"They're His laws!"*

Somewhat dismayed, Jacob hurries back to his documents.

"Every prophecy foretold was fulfilled." Jacob comments, "If Aldebaran was visible..." Jacob pauses, "Of course, *'Aleph'*—

"Symbolizing *God*," Zac interjects.

Jacob quickly adds, "And the 't' shaped Cross, now representing *'Tav'* would contextually translate as *upon the cross*. Yes, Aleph and Tav, *God upon the cross*, there for all the world to see!

Nick states, "Aleph... and Tav?"

"Yes, in Greek, the Alpha and Omega, but in Hebrew, aleph vav tav, the very claim of Christ in the book of Revelation! The very thought, I mean..." Jacob looks at Zac and bemoans, "How could they miss the signs, so many signs?"

Zac's cynicism wells up, "Maybe they didn't."

Jacob concludes, "Maybe? They didn't. Remember, the chief priests were complaining to Pilate to change what he had written and placed above the Cross." He becomes emphatic, "That sign was said to have contained the tetragrammaton, YHVH, thus declaring Christ as God's sacrificial offering for sin...God, Himself." Angered, Jacob sharply indicts, *"Oh, no, they saw it, all of it, and proceeded to keep it secret for all these years!"*

"So, maybe there's a connection?" Nick cautiously interjects.

Jacob's exhilaration heightens his sudden annoyance with Nick. He looks at Zac. "He's your friend...do something."

Seeing Nick's frustration, Zac attempts to explain, "To the Nazis, Aldebaran had a totally different meaning."

"Capisce?" Jacob sharply interjects. He grabs another document. "Look, these are plans for a peace time space program. The Nazis seemed dead set on reaching the Aldebaran System." He chuckles, "They honestly believed it part of their destiny."

The Sergeant is nervously pacing when he feels a chilling draft. "Why does it feel so—?" Suddenly face to face with a wooden gargoyle, he is momentarily startled. "Creepy?"

Zac casually replies, "Probably because the Nazis were heavy into séances, you know, talking to dead spirits, ancient occult writings, stuff like that." His words are anything but reassuring to the Sarge.

Jacob reacts, "Fools! They persisted despite horrible encounters with beings." He turns the page. "It's as if—" Jacob is stunned by what he sees. "Zac, some of the missing."

Zac quickly flips page after page, the document cites countless victims with I.V.'s of fluids going in, while their blood is slowly drawn out.

Jacob speculates, "They look comatose, like they were being prepared for long term blood production." Zac looks towards the star chart.

Nick rushes to view the photos. "You mean like for a journey?"

Zac slowly walks towards the star map. "A very long journey." He notices a date, November 3rd, scrawled on the map.

Nick and Jacob look at each other, then at Zac.

"You mean for food? Nick doesn't know what to think. "C'mon, the Nazis weren't vampires...were they?"

Jacob turns, overlooking the absurdity of the question, he states matter-of-factly, "Well, technically, you're not born a vampire, you become one."

All look at Jacob, and then at each other.

Zac looks at Jacob and recalls, "Nick called Mr. Beck a werewolf, you're talking vampires."

"Where's this all leading to?" Nick looks at a wide-eyed Sergeant then at Zac and Jacob. "I mean, are we looking for a room full of coffins now?"

A deep thump is heard as the room momentarily shakes causing the Sergeant to clutch his weapon. "For the love of Pete! Would ya hurry it up, already?"

Zac raises a quieting hand while he scans a global map. "Wait, the Nazis believed this Aryan super race originally thrived in a colder climate. We're talking polar cold."

"This is good!" Nick gets excited. "They say some Nazi Admiral went nuts at the Nuremberg trials, shouting about an "invulnerable" fortress in the ice. Sounds like you're on the right track, but which pole? We only have one shot at this."

Zac explains, "This Aryan homeland was originally thought to be at the North Pole."

The jittery Sergeant blurts out, "That settles it. Let's get outta here!"

"Not so fast." Zac turns and scours the map once more. "They also believed some sort of polar shift made the Antarctic their new homeland."

"Antarctica?" Jacob injects, "That's one of the said locations of Atlantis."

"And...?" Nick queries.

Jacob turns his attention to Nick, "Home of the so-called Gods of Atlantis, the Watchers, Fallen Angels...the Nephilim." He murmurs, "Zac, the blood... The Nephilim were said to have developed a taste for blood...and cannibalistic tendencies."

There's a long pause as all stand stunned.

Zac shrugs. "Well, okay, that's it!" Our U-boat is headed for the Antarctic. It shouldn't be too hard for you to—"

Zac stops mid-sentence as he hears Nick chamber a round. "I'm afraid this does change things, for you and the Professor." Nick sits halfway onto the table. Pleased with their findings, he relaxes for a moment. "Dr. Gomes, you are good! A rendezvous in the Antarctic? Sounds perfect. Airman Popper and I were wondering if our little surprise party was ever going to happen."

Zac and Jacob look at each other in utter bewilderment.

Zac presses, "Who do you work for?"

Nick smirks. "Don't worry about that. Your skills and the Professor's may be needed to decipher any symbols we find...in the Antarctic. And I really can't take no for an answer, so I'm not asking."

Zac shrugs hoping to ease the tension. "No problem. Just send us anything—"

"You know there's no time for that." Nick interrupts. "You're coming with us."

Zac becomes belligerent. "Listen, we're civilians now." Gesturing towards Jacob, he adds, "archeologists, not soldiers!"

"Think of the Ark." Nick reminds Zac.

"Are you shanghaiing us?" Zac's suspicions about Nick fuel his anger. "The war's over, captain!"

Nick gives hint of his true mission, "My orders are to bring an end to a very real threat, at any cost...no matter the cost."

"Orders?" Zac is demanding. "Do you really believe there are Nazis living at the Poles just waiting to launch a counterattack?"

Jacob's chuckling catches their attention.

Zac and Nick, react in unison, "*What?*"

An amused Jacob raises his hands and smiles. "I don't believe the captain's involvement is merely by chance." He looks at Nick. "You planned on meeting Zac. You knew I was arriving, and why."

Nick pauses then gestures as if to weigh his options. "Okay, we'd been following Mr. Beck for some time. When you sent that package, I was assigned to it, to observe and report. I didn't—"

"*You were spying on me?*" Zac, already agitated, confronts Nick.

"Not exactly," as Nick explains, he turns his head towards Jacob then slowly back. "I was more looking out for—"

Zac delivers a solid right, catching Nick off guard. The Sergeant takes a quick step towards Zac, but Nick raises his hand.

Zac chides Nick, "Were you looking out for that?"

As Nick rubs his jaw, he explains.

"Look, I could get life in prison for what I'm about to tell you. By the way, thanks for the confirmation. We needed to be sure we didn't have to worry about the Arctic too. Our allies were first to track the Nazis down to the Antarctic but all we got were tales of strange creatures and insurmountable forces. A few years later, an armada under the guise of a polar exploration was sent."

The Sergeant eagerly adds, "Can you believe it? An armada of military ships and the press bought it!" He laughs. "It even made National Geographic!"

Nick continues, "Anyway, story is they were beaten back. Details are classified but the threat was real enough that some recommended the use of atomic bombs. Serious enough for you?"

A dumbfounded Zac sarcastically remarks, "Good thing I'm still packed."

The tip of the pendulum has been slowly rising towards the door. The door creaks, catching everybody's attention, then slams shut.

The Sergeant, in a panic, rushes over and pulls with all his might. "Oh-no-you-don't!" He slowly forces the door open. His eyes widen as he gazes into the darkness. Something is rising and getting louder.

All feel a strong draw towards the doorway. Zac shouts at the Sergeant, *"Get back! Get away from—"*

"Auugh!" Too late, the Sergeant is yanked, grappling hook and all, out of the room and into the darkness.

A deep, deafening drone fills the air as dog tags, watches and weapons drag all towards the doorway. Zac realizes the castle tower has become magnetized. He shouts, *"Drop your metal, all of it!"*

Nick grunts, "Not...my...gun!"

While struggling, all hear something grinding its way up the dark stone walls, something immense. Suddenly, there is complete silence, as their terrifying tug-of-war abruptly ends. All tumble to the floor.

A sudden whooshing sound draws the air from the room as they all now struggle to breathe.

Nick gasps. *"Air, what's happening...to the air?"*

As if the castle itself had drawn a massive breath and released it, a powerful blast of air roars back, through the doorway, flinging all, like rag dolls, against the wall.

The Sergeant is suddenly blown back into the room. He slams into some low hanging artwork, knocking a trove of hidden documents loose. Caught by the endless rush of air, the documents swirl all about the room.

Pinned against the walls, the others helplessly watch as a huge disk rises past the doorway, snapping the wooden steps on its way up. As the disk passes, the whirlwind subsides.

Zac rushes to the doorway and finds that their only means of escape is gone. He follows the splintered steps as they tumble downward. From far below, he spies the dim glow of muffled explosions. With a growing rumble, the castle begins to slowly sink.

Nick rushes to the doorway. Realizing their predicament, he weighs the situation. "Exploding charges, tower collapsing, no way out." He turns to Zac, "you take this one."

Zac grumbles, "I got the last one!" He looks around, then points. "The window!"

Nick draws his gun but hesitates, seeing that the stained-glass window is a depiction of the Crucifixion. Zac becomes emphatic, "*It's the only way!*" Seeing Jacob smiling, he points a cautionary finger. "Don't you start!"

Nick flips his gun's safety off and shoots away the glass. As Jacob helps the stunned Sergeant to his feet, Zac takes and shoves a grappling hook into the launcher. He takes aim through the shattered window, and fires.

The Private sits in the truck, calmly reading a comic book when he is suddenly jarred back to reality by the hook's violent arrival. It rips through the canvas roof, shattering the windshield in its grab for the windshield's frame.

Zac quickly attaches the line to the struts on the flying wing.

"What...?" As the Private struggles to adjust the cracked rearview mirror, he glimpses the slack on the rope. "*I knew it, I knew it!*"

Being parked on a downward slope, the truck has been left in gear. The private turns the key, lunging the truck forward before it stalls. He suddenly remembers. "*Oh, yeah!* 1st gear, clutch in!" This time, when the Private simultaneously pushes the clutch in and starts the truck, it slowly begins to roll forward. "Man, that's slow!"

Still pressing on the clutch, the Private grabs the gear shift and thrusts it forward. The truck backfires, then, coincidently, starts to roll a little faster. "Still too slow... 3rd gear!" The Private pops the clutch, jerking the truck forward, which yanks the rope taut. The truck again stalls.

A deep rumbling makes him look in the rearview mirror where he sees stones falling from the castle tower. Panicked, he jumps from the truck. "Oh, no!" He quickly paces about as he self-deprecates, *"You broke the castle."* Turning towards the castle he loudly laments, *"SORRY!"* Hurrying back to the truck, he murmurs, *I'm dead, I'm dead!"*

In the castle, the swaying of the tower and falling debris are making it difficult for Nick to loop a harness around Jacob. He yells to Jacob, *"Hang on!"*

"Yes, yes." Jacob replies in a dismissing voice.

Jacob slides down to safety. The floor begins to splinter and collapse as Nick pushes the dazed Sergeant through the window and towards safety.

As Nick prepares to glide, he grabs a satchel of documents and shouts above the rumbling, "Zac!"

"Right behind you!" Zac yells.

As Nick nears the back of the truck, the constant tugging finally yanks the flying wing from the ceiling. It flips onto the table, landing struts up. The slack rope causes Nick to lose his grip. He plop flat on his back, just shy of the truck.

Seeing the slack rope on the floor, Zac turns and runs towards the flying wing just as the center of the floor crumbles beneath him. Falling, he drops into a lower chamber, and is horrified at the sight of scores of bodies, drained, with I.V.'s still in their arms.

The chamber floor crumbles, dropping the dead and Zac. At the last second, he grabs hold of the dangling grappling line. As he swings helplessly over the black abyss, the tower emits an eerie groan as it tilts. The walls surrounding the window begin to crumble. The roof begins to fall away, dropping debris all around Zac, threatening to break his grip.

Seeing the slack line, Nick barks orders to the Private, "Let's go, move forward! *Hurry!*"

The Private grinds gears and pops the clutch. The truck charges forward, but again stalls.

The trucks forward motion yanks Zac back up into room and drags the wing from the table. It now stands, nose straight up and straddling the elongated hole in center of the floor.

While the Private anxiously cranks the stalled engine, Zac inches his way towards the wing and grabs the support struts. The truck roars to life.

The frenzied Private unwittingly finds a gear while gunning the engine. Instantly, the truck plows forward, yanking the flying wing and Zac straight up and away as the doomed tower collapses.

The Private brakes as a surprised Zac, facing backwards, glides. Nick and the Sergeant quickly begin wrapping the excess line around a gun mount.

"*Go, go!*" Nick yells at the Private, then at Zac, "*Hang on Zac!*"

Getting the hang of things, the Private sends the truck racing.

"*Whoah! Get me down!*" Zac hates heights.

Nick and the Sergeant begin reeling Zac in.

Nick shouts to the Private, "*Slow down!*" The Private hits the brakes and the flying wing dips, causing Zac to grip the struts hard.

Seeing Zac's predicament, Nick barks at the Private, "*No, faster, much faster!*"

The frenzied Private misses 1st gear but finds 2nd and floors it. The engine winds up before shooting the truck forward and springing Zac higher.

The flying wing yaws wildly, then takes a sudden dip. Grazing a power line, sparks fly as the wing begins to smoke.

Zac gives an emphatic shout, *"GET-ME-DOWN!"*

"What'd he say?" Jacob asks.

"I think he said he can see the town?"

The Sergeant's comment has Nick looking puzzled, while Jacob just stares at the Sergeant.

The Private speeds on, turning, and occasionally sliding the truck all around the castle grounds, trying to keep Zac airborne while Nick and the Sarge reel him in. Just as Zac is pulled to within reach of the truck, the wing bursts into flames.

Nick leans out, straining to grab Zac's boot when the truck suddenly hits a bump that sends Nick soaring. He snags Zac's boot, but the added weight slowly brings the flying wing down causing Nick's feet to drag on the ground.

The truck careens past a muddied warning sign and crashes through a locked gate. It leaps onto a downward slopping road and straight towards a boat launch and lake.

The Private slams the brakes, causing Nick to lose grip and bounce hard off the ground and into stacks of bundled ropes and tarps.

The combination of Nick releasing Zac's boot and the truck braking causes the flying wing to catapult over the truck in a long half-circle.

Zac finally loses his grip. *"Whooaahhh!"* Zac soars up and over in a long, slow backwards summersault, across the lake. The burning wing finishes its half-circle and nosedives into the water, hissing and smoldering.

Zac hits the water feet first and plunges through a hole in a sunken German bomber. Jostled loose, skeletons drift towards their visitor. Zac's adrenaline-fueled escape has him springing free and swimming to shore in record time.

Exhausted, Zac wades past the smoldering wing and up the boat ramp. Jacob, grinning from ear to ear, hands him his hat. Nick and the Sarge roar with laughter at Zac's acrobatics.

Nick catches his breath. "That was quite a show! But I don't think they make a merit badge for kite gliding. Might catch on, though, *Ha!*"

Zac limps towards the Private, still sitting in the half-submerged truck. The Private sheepishly pretends to adjust the rear-view mirror when it breaks off in his hand. Zac stops and leans in. "First time, eh? You're a natural."

As the Private smiles up at Zac, his view is drawn further up. His jaw drops as a huge shadow covers all. Looking up, Zac is awe-struck by an enormous disk silently hovering over the castle. The sight of Nazi insignias brings a collective chill down their backs. Suddenly, from every direction come other disks, six in all. They pause only for a moment before quickly accelerating in a southerly direction.

The Sergeant turns a blind eye. "Nope, didn't see a thing."

Nick mutters in disbelief, "So it's true." He's also struck by a fearful possibility. "Zac, did we do that?"

"I don't believe it." Jacob remarks.

Zac comes to his own frightening conclusion. "That's how they beat the Armada. Hitler's Redoubt is coming true."

"I don't believe it!" Jacob becomes obstinate.

Taking a deep breath, Zac sighs, "Believe it, Jacob. This time, believe it."

Nick hurries to the truck. "I've got to report this!"

"No!" Zac stops Nick. "Don't tip our hand. They're heading south, just like us."

"But... Then, let's go!" Nick eagerly states.

The Sergeant verbalizes his objection while all clamor onto the truck, "Oh no, town pub for me. Y'all have a nice trip and gosh it all, be sure to write. On second thought, don't wanna know."

The B-17's engines roar to life. Destination, the Azores and back to the B-47.

CHAPTER 12

◆——————◆

N EARING THE AZORES, it quickly becomes a rough ride as the flying fortress is battered by winds from a fierce night storm.

Nick shouts, "Strap it tight and high hold on!"

Lightning reveals the runway coming up fast as Nick and Zac grip the controls. Suddenly one engine is struck. Cockpit lights flicker as they bounce hard against the tarmac. The B-17G races down the runway while Nick and Zac frantically stab down on the well-worn brakes. Sirens can be heard as the fortress rolls to a stop. All are surprised when military police, leaping and shouting incoherent commands, surround the old war bird.

Through the deluge, Airman Popper watches from beneath the B-47 while Nick and the others are unceremoniously shoved into a panel truck.

Anxious to reunite, he begins to approach but is stopped cold when a sharp-eyed Nick discreetly gestures a command to Mike, who nods and hurries back to the B-47. A policeman waves his gun, and all vehicles quickly speed away.

Rushed down a darkened hallway and up a flight of stairs, they are shoved into a room occupied by a seemingly anxious, but definitely impatient officer and his entourage.

"Americans!" The short, highly decorated, and highly frustrated General struts. In near perfect English, he barks his displeasure, "You think you can just do as you please, come and go as you please, without consequence! I have a client! That plane is my responsibility. You were not authorized to take it!"

Zac mumbles to Nick, "I thought you said—"

"Look..." Nick interrupts, "General, sir, I distinctly requested you be notified."

"Wait, client? Zac has questions, "What client?"

The General shoots his hand up, silencing Zac, then wags a finger before touching the side of his nose. "So, perhaps an oversight?" The General ponders his options. "Nevertheless..." He turns to the guards as he addresses our trio, "Protocol will be followed." Smiling, he barks at the guards, "Our best accommodations, pronto!"

"You see?" Jacob smiles. "No need to worry."

Nick and Jacob sit, staring at the rusty bars, while Zac lies on a metal bed frame, chewing on a piece of straw.

Jacob puts his handkerchief over his nose to block the stench before commenting, "Really? Two weeks to notify the Embassy?"

Nick complains, "We haven't got two days." He looks over at Zac. "Are you going to just lie there?"

"I'm thinking."

That's not good enough for Nick. "C'mon Zac, you're always breaking into places, tombs and stuff."

"Mostly into, not out of."

"Well, how 'bout pretending to break into the room on the other side of those bars?"

Lightning gives Zac an idea. He jumps up and begins dismantling the bed frame.

"Atta boy, Zac!" Nick's enthusiasm is short lived. "Uh, what's he doing?"

Jacob shrugs.

A busy Zac instructs Nick and Jacob, "Give me your belts." Zac wedges a bed frame bar onto the cell's door. He tightly lashes the other bar and pushes it out their cell window and into the rain. They wait.

Nick grows impatient. "Now what?"

Zac remains quiet, seemingly self-assured.

Seeing what Zac is up to, Jacob advises, "The storm is moving away."

Zac hurries towards the commode. "We need a better conductor." Zac fills a cup with water from the toilet. Spilling some along the way, he managers to pour most of it over the metal bars. The others are slightly grossed, but join in with their prison-issued cups. They wait.

Again, Nick grows inpatient. "Well?"

Less self-assured, Zac forces an air of confidence as he states, "We wait."

Jacob notes, "The storm is still—"

"Alright, back away!" Zac grumbles as he reaches up and pulls the bulb housing down. Sparks fly as he yanks the housing off and pulls the excess wire through the ceiling. Nick and Jacob squint in tense anticipation as Zac touches the wires to a bar.

A lightning bolt explodes into the room, throwing all back and blasting the cell door open. The lightning quickly tracks through the spilled water and explodes the toilet bowl. Suddenly, high pitched squeals are heard, echoing down the hallways. Swirling clouds of steam spew from every cell amid shouts and moans." The accusations fly.

"*What did you do?*" Nick takes a disciplinary tone.

"*Me?*" Zac quickly takes issue, "*You were the one that wanted out so badly!*"

Nick retorts, "*I didn't say wake the whole prison!*"

Jacob charges between them and towards the exit. Zac and Nick stop their bickering and follow his lead. From every cell they pass, prisoners are seen stomping about, while others stand soaked. The chaos spurs our trio to run all the faster.

They emerge running from the jail amid shouts and curses coming at them in a variety of languages.

Airman Popper has fired-up the B-47. He frantically gestures them to hurry as sirens blare their escape. The pop and flash of fast approaching gunfire drives Nick to push the slow-moving B-47 full throttle.

With what seems like the whole police force catching up to them, Nick hits the rocket-assist take-off, driving the B-47 skyward with a hard kick felt by all.

A huge cloud of smoke envelopes and disorients their pursuers. Some brake hard and spin on the wet tarmac, producing multiple chain-reaction crashes as the B-47 roars away.

From a window, a silhouetted figure watches the chaos as the mighty Stratojet disappears into the night sky. Behind the intruder, a swinging bulb reveals a smoking luger and the General lying in a pool of blood. The mystery figure turns to light a cigarette, then picks up the phone. "They are on their way." Before leaving, he looks into a mirror and adjusts his eyepatch.

CHAPTER 13

THE MORNING LIGHT sees the B-47 on course, heading south at top speed. Zac and Jacob look at each other, having not forgotten that they have been, technically, shanghaied. Jacob shrugs. Zac nods as both quickly immerse themselves in a treasure of documents. Zac makes a startling discovery, "Why are all these in English?"

He quickly shuffles through them and comes to a disturbing realization. "These are post-war plans to infiltrate governments." Turning a page, his sudden suspicions are confirmed. "With political saboteurs!"

He slowly attempts to peel apart the documents that landed with him in the lake. "Whoever wrote these was just learning English."

Jacob has the same problem. "This too, can't read... No, wait!"

He is suddenly shocked, unwilling to believe what he's reading. "They plan to exterminate whole countries, enslaving millions for blood production! But why, why so much blood?"

Mike speaks out of turn, "Hey, Nick, it's a good thing we—"

"Let's keep the channels clear." Nick quickly interrupts.

Zac sees Nick's attempt to shut up the young navigator.

"By the way, I don't know much about planes, but I don't think you have enough fuel to fly all the way to the Antarctic. I do recall reading something about a B-47, with a nuclear payload, going down in this area. Story is, it failed to rendezvous for refueling, presumed lost at sea or something."

Nick pauses, contemplating his response. "No, we made it."

Zac stretches back, almost gloating, he folds his arms. "Why am I not surprised?"

Nick decides to bring Zac and Jacob up to speed.

"Strictly speaking, that story back in Germany put you and the Professor at a higher security level, so... Orders were to carry two nukes; make it look like they were lost at sea, in the event they were needed. You know, plausible deniability. It was—"

"Plausible deniability?" Zac abruptly interrupts. "So, the President... Who do you work for?"

Nick is quick to clarify, "The Secret Service protects the President, we protect the country."

Zac presses further. "Alright, so where did you disappear to?"

Nick looks out his window. "Down there, Ascension Island."

They land on what was once a strategic airbase during World War II. As they roll to a stop, the base comes to life. A jeep carrying heavily armed soldiers rushes up to the B-47. Zac and the others emerge as the soldiers exact a perimeter. A lumbering cargo truck slowly brakes as ground crews begin the dangerous task of loading two miniaturized 'nukes' while others commence refueling.

The ground crew foreman approaches Nick. "We'll have 'er ready by morning."

Nick objects, "Negative, we leave as soon as is possible."

Zac emerges. Flexing a stiff arm, he asks Nick, "Where exactly are we?"

Nick sees no need to get too specific, "Somewhere between Africa and Brazil. Stretch your legs, but don't go too far. We have appointments to keep." Nick smiles and shifts his focus to the ground crew. He begins to chat with the foreman, "You're new here?"

The foreman leans on the B-47. "Yeah, got in yesterday." Suddenly, a support fails. Nick rushes to keep one crewman from being crushed. As others rush to their aid, the foreman walks away. Without breaking his stride, the foreman opens his lunch box and quickly checks a makeshift timer and explosives.

Zac strolls towards rocky shoreline. From a distance, he spies Nick, now fumbling with several small boxes. A woman approaches and embraces Nick while several small children dance around. He points and they eagerly rush to open their gifts.

Zac sits, rubbing his new scar.

Jacob approaches. "Do you want to talk about it?"

Zac hesitates. Looking out to sea, he asks, "What did you see?"

"I saw one taken and one left behind."

Jacob's remark, prompts a sarcastic response from Zac, "Which one was I?"

Jacob smiles. "I guess it wasn't your time."

Zac questions Jacob's assumption, "I thought you had to really...you know, believe?"

"I don't recall God needing our permission. What puzzles me is how the Ark remained hidden for so long. I mean, the Romans mined all over that area."

"That's it!" It suddenly all falls into place for Zac. "The crack in the rock, it was the perfect plan." Jacob's hesitation causes Zac to add, "Maybe?"

Jacob ponders, *"'The earth quaked, and the rocks rent'."*

Zac suggests, "So, maybe it wasn't a minor detail?"

Jacob retorts, "Since when is anything in the Bible a minor detail?" Pondering Zac's query, Jacob quizzes him, "What's the first rule when mining limestone?"

Zac sees where Jacob is going. "Avoid areas with cracks. Limestone hardens when it's cut and exposed to the air. Any cracks were always passed over." Zac grasps the import of his comment, "Avoid areas with cracks! Of course, the crack would've protected the Ark."

"While the Romans protected their quarry." Closing his eyes, Jacob briefly enjoys a sweeping sea breeze.

Zac's enthusiasm wanes, "Hold on, the Romans mined way before the crucifixion. That means the crack would've already been there!

Jacob pulls out his handkerchief. Wiping away the ocean's mist, he reminds Zac, "Solomon did mine there first. Later, workmen actually did find such a seam of bad rock, as it were, and dug around it!" Jacob pauses. "In time, what was left had the appearance of a skull... Jeramiah's Grotto, Golgotha or Calvary, as some call it. Perhaps Solomon chose that particular spot to place the Ark beneath. Perhaps Solomon created the crack, in proximity to the Temple. By the time the Romans arrived, they would have also disregarded that spot but still protected their quarry."

Taking Jacob's assessment as confirmation, Zac stands confident. "The perfect plan."

Jacob catches his handkerchief on a thorny bush, tearing it. He immediately stands in wide-eyed recollection.

"What is it?" After all these years, Zac knows when Jacob's mind is at work.

Jacob becomes animated, thrusting his hands upwards then slapping his hands together in excitement. *"And, behold,*

*the veil of the Temple was rent in twain from top to the bottom and
the earth did quake, and the rocks rent..."*

Zac becomes intrigued. *"Rent... Same word... Same
meaning?*

"Don't you see? By utilizing the primary form of the verb
'rent' allowed for simultaneous messaging." Barely able to
contain his enthusiasm, Jacob steps back and settles on some
driftwood.

He continues, "When there was a death in the family, only
the father was permitted to rent his garments, specifically, to
tear his outer garments, in mourning, from top to bottom."
Jacob speaks with an eagerness, "Zachary, the Temple veil
was called *the hem of Yahweh's robe*, God's outer garment!
During the crucifixion, it would have been obvious, but
especially to those in the Temple area, and, might I say, a
bit terrifying."

Overwhelmed by Jacob's revelations, Zac hesitates.
Posturing, he then gestures, "That's some messaging.
Counting the one preached, that makes two." Zac nervously
makes a sarcastic and seemingly disjointed remark, "Better
than Morse code."

"Samuel Morse...Samuel!" Jacob is, again inspired,
"Zachary, my boy, that's it!"

"What, another message?" Zac is still reeling from
Jacob's revelation.

Jacob becomes elated, "Indeed! *Yes*, to those at the
Temple... *Yes*, it would have been so clear. The prophet,
Samuel, when King Saul grabbed and tore the hem of his
robe, Samuel declared, *"The LORD has rent the kingdom of
Israel from you today, and has given it to one of your neighbors -
to one better than you."* Jacob slaps his hands together and
laughs, "How's that for a multifaceted message?"

"Neighbors?" Zac's delivers a cautious response.

"Who are the closest neighbors, theologically speaking, to the Jews?" Jacob prompts.

"Christians?" Zac suddenly realizes that his quick answer is a game-changer.

The weight of Jacob's revelations only seems to energize him. "In the darkest moment in history, God proclaimed the Old Covenant ended and the New Covenant begun." He quickly adds a solemn caveat, "Lest we forget, God's promises to his people remain. With their country restored, I believe the best is yet to come!"

On his way to fathoming the depths of Jacob's discourse, Zac finds himself remaining a bit apprehensive, "This is too much. I mean... I suppose all this was necessary—"

"Necessary? My dear boy, remember, *without the shedding of blood, there is no forgiveness of sins.*" Jacob eagerly recounts, "Yes, *'the rocks rent'*... Zachary, during sacrifices, blood was only sprinkled on one side of the Ark. The other side was preserved for the Messiah. A perplexing command, impossible to comprehend, until now."

Zac stands confused as his mind races, "But the rocks... rent, in pain?"

Jacob ponders before hazarding a correlation, "Yes, the very earth, renting, creating a way to the Ark, to receive His blood."

Zac's questions keep coming, "Wait, I thought Christ presented His blood in heaven."

Jacob sharply retorts, "Really? Do you even own a Bible? *'He bowed the heavens and came down; the Lord is in His holy temple; the Lord is on His heavenly throne.'* The Ark and heaven, it's where they met...waiting...all this time, below the crucifixion site!"

Jacob quietly recalls, "There is also a little regarded story about Christ's mother, who, as a young maiden, helped sew the great veil that was torn, in a sense, making it her own.

Perhaps…it could be said that, in some small way, the Father bore her sorrow with His.

"Hold on. This is..." Zac hesitates. "How has all this been overlooked?" Zac's analytical training and demanding of evidence, betrays his lack of faith. "We need proof."

"*Ha*…rising from the dead wasn't enough?" Jacob's sarcasm has grown sharp.

Zac remembers the package sent to him for safe keeping. "What exactly did you find when you examined the blood?"

Jacob bullishly states, "Proof!" He attempts to explain, "You know, His ways—"

"Hold on… I'm sorry." Zac suddenly realizes he's being caught up in Jacob's enthusiasm. "Let's get one thing straight, I didn't sign up for some… One of your crusades!" Jacob waxes philosophical, "Fate has us don many hats. Who's to say—"

"See this hat?" Interrupting, Zac speaks unequivocally, "I'm very fond of this hat. If it's the only one I ever wear, that's fine by me."

Jacob presses. "Circumstances change, even facts."

"Truth, facts, what's the difference?" Zac grows cantankerous.

"Well, back in the tunnel, what exactly happened?"

Zac stands silent.

"Well?" Jacob is determined to get an answer.

Zac hesitates as he dares to recall, "I thought I died." Zac turns, caught off-guard by his emotions. "Why me?"

"You know, a little faith—"

Zac quickly snaps back. "Too many chiefs. Some say better taken, some, better left behind."

Jacob folds his hands in expectation. "And now, what do you say?"

Zac leans into Jacob and sarcastically begs the question, "Which one was I?"

Jacob hesitates before touching on a tender subject. "Your mother once said that truth was the only gift mankind wrapped upon receipt. In rituals, and mind you, of both the scientific as well as religious." He quietly reminisces. "I'd forgotten your mother's wisdom. Zac, do you remember?"

Zac's silence tells Jacob that it might be best to elaborate on the more pertinent topic. "What if the Ark were, let's say, allowed to be stolen. What if we are being led to some final confrontation?"

Zac stares out to sea as Jacob continues, "And, what if your wound is a mark, a choosing, of sorts? I agree, one wound does not a Stigmata make, but such a mark—"

"Alright, already! You made your point. This is way too preachy for me."

Children noisily rush towards them and point to a distant, shouting Nick, *"Come on! We're burning daylight!"*

Jacob smiles and opens his arms to the children.

Looking towards the B-47, Zac spies a nervous-looking foreman shove a package into the rear compartment of their jet, then hop into a truck and speed away.

Zac is suddenly gripped with fear. He runs while motioning and yelling to Nick, *"Look out!"* He frantically points, *"There!"*

A puzzled Nick looks from side to side.

"Behind you!" Zac yells again.

Nick finally opens the compartment, revealing dynamite and a ticking timer. With only seconds to spare, he disarms it.

Zac sees the foreman speeding down a dirt road. *"There he goes!"*

Zac and Nick, still holding the bomb, run towards a jeep where Mike is napping. Without breaking his stride, Nick shouts, *"Mike!"*

A groggy Mike answers, *"Yessir!"*

"Follow that truck!"

Gunning the motor, Mike speeds off, leaving Nick and Zac slack-jawed.

Nick and Zac both shout, "*MICHAEL!*"

Mike hits the brakes and backs up. "Sorry, sir."

Careening over an embankment they spot a seaplane and its occupants preparing to depart. Mike hits the gas and in seconds all three are jumping out, ready for a fight. They quickly advance on the pilot who slowly emerges from the plane. Rising to full stature, he reveals an imposing physique, along with a loaded pistol crossbow. Zac, Nick, and Mike raise their hands.

The foreman emerges from his truck. Removing his coveralls, he reveals an S.S. uniform. Drawing a luger, the Nazi displays a sinister smile as he strolls up to our trio. "Lately, nothing's been going as planned. Hmm...what to do? Yes, now one of us will have to fly with you, and one of you will have to...remain. But which one."

The Nazi ponders, as he slowly walks past Zac, Mike, and Nick. "Let's see, a captain, an airman and a surprise guest. No, wait... FBI, yes?" He backs up to Mike who is standing between Nick and Zac. He looks at Mike's nametag. "Popper? Jewish?"

Mike looks defiantly at the Nazi. "Yes."

Glaring at Mike, he steps away and motions the pilot, who shoots. The arrow strikes deep into Mike's right lung. His knees buckle. Quickly, Nick and Zac take hold of him. With a surge of strength and despite excruciating pain, Mike defiantly stands firm.

Anger rages through Nick and Zac as both step towards the S.S. agent who quickly raises his luger. "He won't die, I'll leave that up to you. I want the activation codes to the bombs."

"What bombs?" Nick plays dumb.

The agent becomes agitated. "Your friend's life ebbs away with every stupid answer." He turns his attention to Zac. "How about you, Mr. FBI?"

"Go ahead...shoot." Zac's contempt is obvious.

The Nazi smiles and gestures towards his luger. "And alert the whole base? I think not."

Inspired, Nick and Zac look at each other, then charge, surprising the pilot and Nazi. The pilot quickly aims at Zac and fires, but Mike jumps in front and is struck again.

Zac cries out, *"No!"* As Zac eases Mikes to the ground, the pilot starts reloading but an enraged Nick charges and delivers a furious right cross, stunning the pilot.

The S.S. agent takes aim as he approaches Zac and the wounded airman. He approaches a little too close. With lightning speed, Zac rises and plants a sharp, upper cut, propelling the S.S. agent who drops his gun.

"That's more like it." Zac relishes the moment.

Nick disappears, leaving Zac to fight the fast approaching pilot. Mike musters the strength to crawl and grab the pilot's leg. When the pilot kicks Mike, Zac retaliates with brutal savagery.

Nick reappears, snatching up the luger, he takes aim. The bloodied pilot and S.S. agent raise their hands. Nick sternly commands, "Go! Leave now."

Zac is dumbfounded by Nick's orders. "What are you doing?" Zac steps towards Nick who quickly point's the gun at Zac, stopping him.

Hearing the seaplane roar off, Nick lowers the gun. Bewildered, Zac challenges Nick, "Whose side are you on?"

Zac hurries to Mike's side, while a vengeful Nick stares at the plane as it quickly climbs. "In about ten sec—" Nick is quickly silenced as an explosion rips the tail off. In flames, the seaplane breaks apart as it cartwheels into the ocean.

While staring at the burning wreckage, Nick wryly comments, "I need a new watch."

Drawn by the explosion, vehicles approach from every direction. Zac stuffs a handkerchief into Mike's wounds but can't stop the bleeding.

Mike struggles for air. *"Sorry I couldn't help...(Panting). Nick says I...could'a been a pretty good boxer...(Coughing)."*

Zac places his hand under Mike's head. "Why'd ya do it, kid—? No, don't try to talk!" Zac hides his despair as he watches Mike's blood soak into the sand.

Mike gathers his remaining strength but can only stammer, *"(Gasping)...My step-brother told me...just don't die for nothin'...and you're pretty important to the mission."* Unable to do more, Zac hides his frustration by encouraging the young airman with a smirk, "We're a team. We're all—" Zac stops as Mike's body tenses.

Everybody begins arriving. *"Hurry it up!"* Zac yells.

Jacob finally arrives. He kneels to tend to Mike.

Nick spots a medic. "Corpsman, on the double!"

Mike looks at Nick. *"(Gasping)...Really wanted to make that party."*

"You will, I promise." Forcing a smile, Nick attempts to comfort Mike with an assurance.

Mike suddenly becomes disoriented and grabs Zac's shirt. *"Dad! Tell my dad—"*

"I said stop—" Zac's interruption is silenced when Mike exhales and dies.

Jacob, more than the others, feels the loss of one so young. "Dear God, no."

Zac is speechless.

Nick's eyes well-up. He turns away and spots the radioman in the distance, quickly approaching with the others. *"Blundo!"*

The radioman is an old friend, "Hey, Nick!" The radioman rushes up to Nick but upon seeing Mike's body, becomes more formal, "Yes, sir!"

A somber Nick nods. "Any chatter?" Nick struggles to maintain his composure.

"No, sir…nothing."

Nick turns to Zac. "Good, they didn't get off any messages."

Zac laments, "It should be me."

Doubling his fists in frustration, he looks at Jacob. "What's happening?"

"He was duty-bound, don't take—"

"*No!*" Zac stops Jacob mid-sentence. "Enough." Zac feels a rising despair.

Jacob stands. "Honor him. Don't turn this into some… reckless vendetta. Don't waste his sacrifice."

Zac suddenly rises and dons his hat.

Jacob fears for Zac's sanity as much as for his safety. "What are you going to do? Zachary, vengeance is—"

"*Vengeance?*" Zac snaps, "I'm just going to finish the job."

Nick kneels and gently removes a letter from Mike's uniform.

Zac wryly states, "The party's still on."

Nick looks up towards Zac. "I've got the noisemakers, let's go." As others tend to Mike, Nick pauses at Mike's body and gives a final, heartfelt salute, then walks away.

Zac looks at a mournful Jacob. "I've chased history long enough. It's time I made some of my own." He looks at Mike's body then at the burning seaplane. "Whatever it takes… So help me."

Zac walks away and fails to hear Jacob quietly murmur, "Careful what you pray for."

The flight to the Falklands is quiet. Due to the unofficial nature of the mission, Nick's orders have him landing at a discrete airfield, built miles from any populated area and only feet away from a jagged, rocky shoreline.

All remain onboard during refueling as each wrestle with their grief and the will to press on. The loss of the young Airman causes all to search their souls as each forges a new resolve and urgency towards the mission.

Finally, they are given the 'all clear' to go.

Ahead lies the last leg of their journey, a secret base in the Antarctic. Nick uses the full length of the runway before easing the B-47 up and away. Nick adjusts course and accelerates. The day's events take their toll as Zac and Jacob, grief-stricken and mentally drained, welcome the solace of sleep. The ground crew watches until the roar of the engines gives way to the roar of the ocean.

CHAPTER 14

THROUGH THE ICY waters of the Antarctic, an immense white sperm whale leisurely swims, followed by three females and their pups. When one playful pup speeds off, the immense male gives chase. Both quickly disappear while the others continue their trek southward. From behind a huge ice flow, four immense metal objects glide into their path.

Springing from these puzzling visitors, four smaller objects speedily advance. Whirring through the icy water, they swiftly close in on the curious whales. A hit and one female is killed. The other females instinctively maneuver to protect the pups. The other wire-guided mini-torpedoes select their targets. Another female is killed as the U-boats surge forward. Submerged to periscope depth, frogmen stand poised on all decks. One by one, they fire their harpoons, striking one pup, then another. The last female attacks but is killed by multiple hits.

The massive whale suddenly returns. It charges with a vengeance, broadsiding one U-boat dead center, cracking the hull. The ruptured U-boat struggles to the surface as freezing water rushes in. With klaxons blaring, the captain's eyes widen in horror at the sight of water and sunlight pouring in. He shouts to abandon ship. Panic ensues as the enraged whale leaps repeatedly, slapping down on the thrashing crew. Lungs fill with water, drowning hapless screams. The sea washes over horrified faces as the whale crushes and swallows any attempting to escape.

Finally overwhelmed by the sea, the U-boat founders. The last lingering sound is that from the sinking U-boat's on-deck bell swaying, eerily tolling the ships death knell.

The enraged whale charges the remaining U-boats. Frantically, a sailor fires, but the churning waters send his guided mini-torpedo deep into the sinking hull of the doomed U-boat. A colossal explosion sends a shockwave that stuns the great whale, while a salvo of metal shards pierce its massive body. It is left for dead.

Beck's U-boat approaches just as the others finish securing the whale pups. His U-boat commander offers Beck a view of the carnage through the periscope. "Mr. Beck, have a look at where your next meal is coming from." The U-boat commander broadcasts a reminder to all the U-boats. "Take only the pups. The others will expend too much fuel. Ahead full!" Beck's U-boat maneuvers behind the remaining U-boats and follows.

CHAPTER 15

◆————————————————◆

NICK SPIES THEIR destination, a distant, remote valley surrounded by a treacherous mountain range. A sudden surge of turbulence makes Nick grip the controls and tense his jaw. He muses about the 'genius' who decided to build an airfield here in the first place.

Although it's not his first time here, he's never flown anything as big as a B-47 into it. Another sharp blast of wind threatens to whip the B-47 sideways. Despite fighting the controls every step of the way, he manages a perfect touch down with nary a shudder or a bump.

Rolling down the runway, a row of wrecked and disabled aircraft give testimony to the perilous crosswinds. The sight brings a chill to Nick as the sweat streams down his neck.

While shutting down systems, he looks back at Zac and Jacob, waking, oblivious to the near disaster he has skillfully averted. "Last stop! Smoke 'em if ya' got 'em." He suddenly remembers their deadly cargo. "Belay that, never mind!"

As Zac leaves the B-47, a prayer book and Yamaka drop from behind Airman Popper's seat. He hesitates, then stuffs both in his shirt. Walking, they spot the bombs being wheeled into a tent. Zac spies a familiar looking crate.

All are greeted by the base commander, who motions them towards the mess hall. "Welcome, gentlemen. You're just in time to meet your sub commander and grab a hot meal. By the way, the original commander was yanked at the last minute, For some reason, headquarters seemed eager to get this other guy in. He's a bit eccentric but knows his stuff."

"Sub commander, as in submarine?" Zac glares at Nick.

"Sorry, the Queen Mary was booked." Nick sarcastically retorts.

"I've never been in a submarine." Jacob is excited at the prospect.

Inside the mess hall, the sub's boisterous crew eagerly chows down. The base commander approaches a slight, lone, humble looking figure, seated at the officer's table. He appears enthralled, holding a book in one hand, while supporting an overloaded fork in the other.

"Commander Ben Aharon, this is Captain Nick Desmond, Professor Jacob Malkin and Professor Zachary Gomes.

The base commander suddenly stops and turns. With an inquisitive stare, makes a surprising query, "Say, aren't you the Ark guy?"

"Wrong guy." Zac quietly mutters, *"If I had a dime for every..."* Zac quickly tempers his growing annoyance at the notoriety of this 'Ark' fellow.

Commander Aharon emerges from behind his book. Wearing a monocle, he gestures salutations as he closes a book on Civil War submarine disasters. "Gentlemen, welcome to the end of the world."

All stare at Ben who realizes his poor choice of words. Trying to recover, he thrusts his book towards Zac. "Great book!"

"Thanks, but I'll wait for the movie."

Ben's monocle falls as his eyes widen. *"They're making a movie?"*

Ben's long-time friend and fellow submariner, Ensign Casey, approaches him with a hot water bottle. "Here you go, sir."

Ben is relieved. "Ah, thank you ensign... Ah, yes."

Ben attempts introductions as he adjusts the hot water bottle to his lower back. "May I introduce my right-hand, Ensign Casey." Ben gestures, "Take a gander at our illustrious guests, Captain Nick Desmond, Professor Zachary Gomes and Professor Jacob Malkin." The Ensign snaps a salutes. Nick returns the salute while Zac and Jacob nod.

Zac looks out the window and spies a U-boat being prepared for launch. "Let me guess...that's our ride? I thought we got rid of them all."

The base commander explains, "Mostly, yes. The U-234 was one of Germany's largest subs. She was at sea, headed for Japan when she surrendered. The two ME262 jet fighters found in her hold were bad enough, but the most disturbing find was the over 500 kilograms of near weapons-grade uranium."

Zac shifts in his seat. "Are you saying we were about to go from an all-out conventional war to an all-out nuclear war?"

Ben adds a disturbing note. "We're not out of the woods yet."

"So, I'm gathering." The unsettling remark draws more of Zac's sarcasm.

A somber Nick sits, seeming troubled, he gazes at Ben. Zac leans towards Nick, but Jacob stops him. "At some point, he who grieves must grieve alone."

The base commander leans back. "Commander Aharon will brief you on the mission."

As all are served a welcomed meal, Ben is caught chewing on a rather large piece of steak. "Mmm, yes, mmm, thank you Commander, and please, if you would all just call me Ben." Ben swallows hard then sips his wine. "Basically, we hope to shadow a U-boat back to its base, get in, blow it up and get out. You are, that is. I'll be in the getaway car."

Ben's seemingly frivolous approach to such a mission brings an uneasiness to Zac. "How long did it take us to come up with that plan?"

"Ah, yes, let's get it all out," Ben retaliates. "I've been briefed on your reputation, Mr. Gomes. Just remember, on my ship, my word is law."

"Gentlemen, please!" The base commander intervenes. Commander...uh, Ben, if you could share some specifics, perhaps..."

"Yes, no time to be ill-mannered." Ben shifts in his chair, seeking a comfortable position. "I apologize. So, intelligence tells us German post-war plans do exist. What they are is where you come in."

Zac, Jacob, and Nick just look at each other.

The base commander brings our trio up to date. "Earlier attempts show their air space to be impenetrable. Ground assaults were disastrous. Any transmissions or communiqués have been nil or undetectable, until now."

Ben tosses a bundle of envelopes towards Zac. "Take a gander at the stamps."

"Clever." Zac is impressed.

He passes some to Jacob who is quick to note similarities. "The names on these envelopes, these are scientists, philosophers, some dead but all with the same ideology."

"Common postage stamps used as hieroglyphics." Zac makes a quick assertion as he hands a bundle to Nick. "One thing is for certain, different stamps from different countries... Same message."

The base commander watches as Nick gingerly handles some blood-stained envelopes and sadly states, "Some were acquired at great sacrifice."

Jacob queries his concern, "But with so many stamps from so many countries..."

"Are we talking a world-wide alert?" Nick queries.

"Maybe," Zac interjects.

"For a world-wide counterattack?" Nick dares to conclude a growing consensus.

Zac quietly hands Jacob one envelope displaying a valuable collector's stamp known as the Bull's Eye. Jacob slowly passes it to Nick who immediately pulls out his coin. It matches. His face becomes flush. Our trio grows silent, afraid to even think of the scope of what may lie ahead.

The sudden silence spurs the base commander to insist, "Gentlemen, please! Is there anything else?"

Jacob adds an ominous observation, "Well, many of these have a recurring theme, symbolizing oneness or one ruler."

"Or government," Nick is quick to add.

Zac discovers a foreboding oddity. "Wait, this stamp is for...the day of the dead."

Jacob turns to Zac. "November 1st? Halloween!"

"Isn't Halloween October 31st?" Nick is confused.

Jacob corrects Nick, "The 31st is the eve of Halloween. Originally, observance lasted from November 1st thru the 3rd."

"But November 1st, that's tomorrow!" Nick exclaims.

The base commander is not given to entertaining flights of fancy and tries to keep everyone focused by asking, "Forgive me, but couldn't that just be a holiday greeting?"

"Not likely." Zac gives all a quick history lesson and an ominous conclusion. "One of Hitler's goals was to replace our holidays with his own. They wouldn't waste the opportunity. Look, this holiday stamp is sliced into three sections. Something's happening on the 3rd." Zac recounts, "November 3rd." He suddenly remembers the date on the map.

Ben soberly narrates, "November 3rd, 1943, Aktion Erntefest... Operation Harvest Festival. The single, largest massacre of Jews in the entire war." Pained, he averts his gaze as the memories flood in. "They began at dawn... By the end of the day, the Nazis had killed over 40,000." He pauses. It is a bitter recollection for Ben as he sardonically remarks, "Some holiday." Ben's gaze falls on every face in the room. "Exactly what are we facing?"

Nick offers a frightening scenario, "Well, there's the missing U-boats, and considering the fact that hundreds of Nazis escaped, including a bunch of doped-up, occult-driven S.S. officers, now possessing an advanced technology, we think that—" The look on everyone's faces stops Nick. He, unconvincingly, attempts to offer some assurance, "But we have the element of surprise."

Ben wryly grins as he offers a devious thought, "An element of horror thrives on surprise."

Nick smiles broadly. "Oh, we have a very big surprise."

Jacob speaks up, "Excuse me...gentleman, about the stamps. The Day of the Dead is a two-day celebration. The first day honors the souls of children; the second, adults."

"Perfect." Zac concludes. "They want the 3rd...? We'll provide the fireworks."

Ben is impressed. "Set the bombs to go off on the 3rd? I like it!"

The Base Commander turns to Ensign Casey. "Ensign, tell them to calibrate the bombs for November 3rd."

Nick attempts to cut the tension with a loud joke. "Hey, Halloween and we're going as a U-boat!"

The whole room becomes a mix of laughter, grumbling and long gazes.

Ben eagerly finishes his chocolate cake and, surprisingly, becomes elated. "Great! I'm beginning to get a good feeling

about this mission. Dr. Gomes, you've proven your worth…
Ha, despite your reputation!"

Zac glares at Jacob who quickly suggests, "I think he has
you crossed with that other fellow."

A sailor comes rushing into the room and hands the
base commander a note. "Gentlemen! This is the break we've
been hoping for… U-boats have been sighted by fishermen!
Commander Aharon, how soon can you be ready?"

Ben quickly downs his wine. "Let's go!"

"*Now*?" The prospects of chasing Nazis in a submarine
does not sit well with Zac.

"What?" Ben smugly notes Zac's hesitancy and jokes,
"Need time to pack?"

As they approach the U-234, Zac spots a newly installed
observation window on the subs conning tower. "Since
when do subs have windows?"

As Ben points, Zac spots Auschwitz prison numbers
tattooed on Ben's forearm, "My idea! The easier to shadow
with. What'dya think?"

"We'll see."

Ben smiles, then nudges Zac, "I know. That's why I put
it in."

As Ben briskly walks away, Zac sighs, "Another
comedian, this is going to be a long trip."

CHAPTER 16

U-234 CUTS THROUGH the icy waters, remaining surfaced for maximum speed. In his assigned, spartan quarters, Zac begins to realize that he's, among other things, a bit on the claustrophobic side. While settling in, a tug on the bedsheets uncovers a well-worn Bible. Hesitating, he finally goes to pick it up when a knock interrupts.

A sailor peers in, "Sir, Ben would like to see you."

He follows the sailor to Ben's quarters where Nick and Jacob are already enjoying a brew.

Another sailor hands Ben his hot water bottle. "Ah, thank you!" Ben whimsically asks as he pours, "How do you like your coffee?"

With no cream or sugar in sight, Zac gathers that Ben is a bit of a prankster. "That's fine, thanks."

Jacob reaches into his pocket and retrieves some hard candy. He plops one into his coffee before offering one to Zac who declines.

"Nick has been briefing me on your plans." Ben states.

Zac sips before sharing his concerns. "I still don't get it. Barely a platoon in Israel, then just two soldiers in Germany. Now we're about to strike a force that's turned back an armada?"

Jacob attempts to reassure Zac, "Fewer numbers have proven their tactical advantage? Look at Gideon or even Sergeant York."

Nick reminds Zac, "Coming in with everything but the kitchen sink didn't work. They won't be expecting us."

Ben is pleased, but has another bad choice of words, "I'm liking the plan. It's the kind they remember you by."

All slowly turn their heads towards Ben who looks puzzled.

"What?"

Nick addresses Zac, "You and Jacob just keep helping with any symbols, we'll do the rest."

Zac notices Ben has a new book, Moby Dick. "Your choice of reading material is not very...reassuring."

"You know how it ends?"

Zac looks at the others and then at Ben. "Are you telling me you never read the story of Moby Dick?"

Ben is almost apologetic, "Well in school they tried to—"

"No, I mean the real story." Zac interrupts.

Ben is intrigued. "He was real? I'm all ears."

Nick laughs. "Oh yeah, a landlubber telling sea lore to a submarine commander. We're all, all ears."

Zac looks intently at Ben. "The story of Moby Dick was based on a real whale, named Mocha Dick—"

"Mocha Dick?" Nick interrupts.

Zac is quick with the sarcasm, "Yeah, named, I suppose, after the Isle of Mocha, off the coast of Chile, not far from here." He gestures Nick, "Do you mind?"

Zac eagerly continues, "*He was the largest whale ever seen... beautiful, white as snow. Still, no fisherman would set sail when Mocha was feeding since he was known to attack and swallow the largest of sharks, whole. But it was not until whalers tried to kill him that he became the terror of the sea. After that, no ship was safe. Scores of battles later, Mocha bore the price of victory with at least a dozen harpoons stuck deep in his back, and a face and body scarred from ramming and crushing scores of ships. Blood ran cold at the very sight of him."* Zac becomes animated. *"Terror chilled the bones of whalers who fought Mocha. They knew they were fighting for their very lives!"*

All eyes are fixed on Zac as he leans back. "It's said he even survived a battle with three whaling ships in a single encounter. Later, he was finally killed, or so they say."

"Ha!" Enthralled, Ben let's known his exhilaration at the tale.

A sailor quickly approaches. "Sir, U-boats!"

"How many?" Ben's tone becomes serious.

"Four, sir!"

Ben's orders resonate through the intercom, "All hands, to your stations, dive, commence shadowing!" Ben excitedly slaps the table, smiles then looks at our trio and gestures, "Gentlemen, shall we?" He rushes off, leaving all to try and keep up. They follow Ben's voice as it echoes down the sub's narrow corridor.

While navigating through the confining corridor, Zac notices Nick is carrying a tool pouch. "So how long you been working with the bomb?"

"About 2 weekends—"

"What!" Startled, Zac blurts out a lightning response.

Nick resumes, "Basically, push this button, don't push that one, and never cut—"

"But!" Zac remains dumbfounded.

Without missing a step, Nick turns and walks backwards as he explains, "Yeah, boxing wasn't really for me, coach said I had two left feet." Nick's head bangs into a hatchway and spills his tools.

Zac delivers a belated, "Look out!"

"Gee, thanks." Nick rubs his head.

"And you're in charge of handling the bombs."

Nick wisecracks, "Must be my two left feet."

Zac makes a snide evaluation, "Mountain goats have two left feet. You don't see them tripping all over the place." Zac continues on, leaving Nick momentarily perplexed.

As Ben approaches, Ensign Casey relinquishes his position at the observation window. Before leaving, Casey points in the direction of the distant U-boats.

Ben nods. "I see 'em." He squints. "That formation dead ahead... *It's moving*? Change course to—" A startled Ben leans back. "Oh, my... *Brace for impact!*" Ben yells as the massive whale charges.

The whale rams them head on, driving U-234 back and into a rock formation. The impact is crippling as the impact damages the torpedo tubes, a propeller shaft and rudder. The great whale is momentarily stunned by the sudden impact.

The sonar operator on one U-boat hears the collision and reports.

The U-boat commander nods and looks through the periscope, but U-234 is obscured by the rock formation and one huge whale. "Just that tenacious whale." The sonar operator has a puzzled look, but the commander is not concerned. "Probably shrapnel, imbedded during the hunt. Carry on."

Numerous leaks from the impact have every available seaman pushed to their limits. As the last leak is plugged, and damage reports arrive, Ben orders U234 closer to the U-boat pack.

Zac rushes in. "What was that?"

"Big fish!" Ben remembers Zac's story and laughs. "*Ha!* It's him, Moby Dick!"

"More like his great grandson." Zac remarks. "Something's got him mad." Ben looks thru his newly installed observation window at the U-boats. "Have a look." Ben shows Zac the U-boats with the dead whale pups lashed to their decks.

Zac quickly spots their target. "There, the one without a whale... *That's Beck.*"

Nick emerges from the torpedo room, wet and exhausted.

Ben asks, "Are the packages O.K.?"

"*Packages?* Who are we kidding?" Ben's downplaying of the power they're carrying does not bode well with Zac.

Nick nervously jokes, "Well, we're still here." Seeing Zac's face, he teases, "You worked for the government; you know how things work."

A cynical Zac responds, "That's what scares me."

CHAPTER 17

S LOWED BY THE damage done to their rudder and propeller, U-234 remains far below and behind the U-boats. They soon catch a break when the U-boats commence maneuvering upwards.

"Ahead slow." Ben gives the command.

Forming a single line, the U-boats begin surfacing one at a time. From the observation window, Ben follows their ascent. Twisting and straining to see, he finally spies the large opening in the ice. "*There*! Commence surfacing." Ben speaks with the cunning of a hunter, "Nice and easy."

During the bloody business of processing of the whale carcasses, U-234 surfaces and docks unnoticed, amid a score of other U-boats.

Ben leads them to the cargo bay where Zac is surprised to see a familiar looking crate. "Is that...? You brought the decoy Ark? Why, or should I ask?"

"Well, to exchange with the real Ark. What'd ya think we were gonna do?" Ben is unaware of Zac's passion for the Ark.

Zac shrugs. "Thought we'd just steal it back."

"Negative." Ben cautions. "The Ark could be found missing at any moment. This will buy us time." Zac appears puzzled. "You know, get in, blow it up and get out." Ben reminds Zac.

"Wait, you mean to blow up the Ark?" Zac fires back.

Ben challenges Zac's sentiment. "The real Ark is what matters, right?"

"But to blow it up?" Zac is flabbergasted.

Jacob quietly comments, "So, once again, the other Ark is to act as a decoy?"

Ensign Casey cautiously enters the conversation, "After, uh, some unique research, they think they've succeeded in combining its power and the bomb's. You know, more bang for your buck."

Jacob laughs uncontrollably, "Is there no end to our arrogance?"

Zac becomes resolute, "You can't blow up the Ark! And who exactly are *they*, anyway?"

"Indeed?" Jacob is quick to add his indignation, "Do you know what you're saying…? That God…that the *Almighty* will be working with you, with us, to destroy the Nazis?"

The ensign shrugs as he calmly states, "Guess you could look at it that way."

A worried Ben adds, "If the Ark performs like I've heard—"

"If this works, we don't want to be anywhere near this place when it goes." Zac quickly finishes Ben's concern with his own.

The U-boat crews hurry ashore, laughing and joking amidst the clamor of the maintenance crews and the butchers harvesting the whale pups. During the commotion, Zac and some of the crew emerge wearing Nazi U-boat uniforms and carrying the Ark onto the dock.

"Just one moment!" A Nazi captain has suddenly arrived, leading a platoon. "We have orders to see this cargo, the Ark, I presume, to its destination."

Zac, surprised to hear English, quickly nods. Thinking fast, he responds, "Your papers, where are they? Come on.

And your English, work on that accent. Listen! You don't hear me with an accent, do you?"

The startled captain fumble for the orders. "No, I mean, yes, I will work on it!"

Zac leans in and presses the point. "No, more casual… *I'll work on it.*"

The captain stammers. "I will. No, I mean…I'll work—"

"Enough! You'll get it…I promise." Zac gives the captain a hardy slap on the back. "Relax, and don't open it."

The captain lets out a nervous laugh. "That's funny. You know the Fuehrer would have my head."

Zac is stunned by the revelation and mumbles, *"The Fuehrer?"*

As the decoy Ark is carried away, Zac's sees the real Ark being lifted out of Beck's U-boat. Gripping the papers, he smiles and motions to the others. "Follow me."

U-boat crewmen finish unharnessing the Ark just as Zac and his crew arrive, "Just one moment! We have orders to see this cargo, the Ark, I presume, to its destination." The Nazi sailor hesitates causing Zac to thrust the orders hard against the sailor's chest and lean into him. "Would you rather your head on a stick?"

The rest of the U-boat crew have been eagerly disembarking when Mr. Beck suddenly emerges, casually chatting with an officer. Zac quickly turns away.

The confused Nazi sailor responds, "Nein! Uh, no! No, I mean, yes, sir!" The sailor motions his crew away, and they eagerly rush to join their comrades. Zac and the others take over and begin heading back.

A wisecracking crewman smiles and remarks, "Hey, that was pretty easy." Zac quickly grabs the crewman's shirt as he draws his fist back, but stops. —*The memory of Airman Popper deserves better*—

Zac lifts a stern finger. "Everything has a price."

CHAPTER 18

A S THE REAL Ark is lowered and stowed, the crew's chatter on deck draws an unexpected visitor. Emerging from the shadows, a lone survivor, a Major Chapman exclaims, "I don't believe it, are you for real?"

Despite his heavy British accent and faded uniform, one young sailor grabs the Major and presses a knife to his neck. The Major spins the sailor to the ground, and deftly puts the knife to the sailor's throat. The Major smiles as he flips the knife and offers it back.

"Major Chapman, at your service!"

The crewmen deliver the Major below deck to Commander Ben and the others. There, a somewhat friendly debriefing ensues.

A cautious Ben starts. "How long have you been here?"

"What year is it?" The Major has questions too.

"1956." Zac suddenly recalls a story circulating about a disastrous British secret mission to the Antarctic.

"Blimey! 6 years!" The Major exclaims.

Suddenly fearing a similar fate, Zac becomes sarcastic, "Well, that's encouraging."

Excitedly looking about at his surroundings, the Major exclaims, "This is great. So, you're scouting? Is the armada waiting for your signal?"

Ben's not yet ready to answer any of the Major's questions. "Pretty remarkable, you surviving all this time?"

A sailor hands Chapman a cup of coffee as the Major replies, "It wasn't easy at first, until I found this sub pen. They keep these boats well stocked. A little here, a little there, so as not to raise suspicion."

An anxious Nick leans in as he focuses on extracting info relevant to the mission. "What can you tell us about any sort of plans?"

The Major puts his coffee down. "You mean, what are you up against? I'm afraid it doesn't look good, ol' boy. The other day, a number of flying disks arrived from the north. The Nazis seemed startled, as if it were unexpected."

Zac, Nick, and Jacob subtly exchange glances.

The Major continues, "Don't underestimate those disks. They go down easy enough, if you can hit them. Their faster than anything."

"What about outside contacts?" Zac leans in. The Major's cheerful demeanor diminishes as he finds himself caught between Nick and Zac's encroaching queries, "Contacts? You just wouldn't believe me. At times, they seem to just appear. Other times, they emerge from these flying disks... hellish creatures."

All are caught off-guard by the Major's shocking comment.

Zac's growing impatience shows. "I meant something more like human sympathizers. Are there any—?"

"Wait a minute! Major Chapman comes to a sudden realization. "Those chaps were loading a crate... Not scouting! You're alone! You're already in the middle of some bloody, stupid plan!"

Just then, a sailor hurries into the room. "Sir, some of the injured, from the collision."

Ben quickly responds, "Yes, does the Major know of any medical facilities?"

CHAPTER 19

D ONNED IN NAZI uniforms, all follow Major Chapman
through the streets of New Berlin. All look about,
amazed at the thriving metropolis, but especially at the
rows of flying disks alongside rooftop missile batteries.
Zac spies the Ark being hoisted onto a tower, well over a
hundred feet above the city.

Nick quietly muses over the insurmountable odds they
may face and musters a flippant remark, "They sure look
like they're getting ready for something big."

Zac continues to watch as technicians' clamp antennae
onto the Ark. "Unbelievable! It looks like they're going to
use the Ark to—"

"What, search for God?" Nick interrupts before joking,
"Maybe they're gonna try to negotiate?"

Zac chuckles, then soberly asks Jacob, "They can't, can
they?"

Laughing as well, Jacob chides the dichotomy, "Well,
let's see, bargaining with the Lord, while in league with the
devil?" Everybody laughs at the absurdity.

Noticing Zac and the other's seemingly mystified at the
abundance of spoken English, Major Chapman volunteers
an explanation, "Years ago, everyone was ordered to learn
and speak only English, to help the saboteurs acclimate."

"Saboteurs?" Zac perks up.

The Major explains, "Not your usual sort. No, these are trained to infiltrate governments. And I don't believe these are the first. How is the world out there, anyway?"

Jacob shrugs and offers a guarded thought, "Cautiously optimistic."

"Except for the occasional war." Nick quickly adds.

"War?" The Major is surprised.

"Between the occasional rumors of war." Zac adds further cynicism.

"Here we are." The Major spies their destination.

While gathering supplies, a shadowy figure draws a Walther pistol from a desk and flips the light switch. Startled, all turn to see a gun pointed at Zac. Hands go up.

Zac grumbles, "Why can't you people point at someone else?"

"Sorry to intrude." A quick-thinking Nick attempts to explain their presence, "Uh, we're explorers... Lost our way, and we have injured."

The figure emerges from the shadows and Zac's jaw drops. "Sarah!"

More curious than defensive, Sarah demands, "Who are you really, and who told you my name?"

Zac takes a deep breath, "Your parents."

Taken aback, Sarah tells the lie she was told, "My parents were killed!"

Zac tries to reassure Sarah, "No...they were in a procession, a lot of people were. All of them looking for missing loved ones."

A sailor, the same one that jumped Major Chapman, has slipped behind Sarah. He lunges, but Sarah skillfully grabs him by the lapels and slams him against the wall, all the while keeping her gun on target. Everyone is surprised at Sarah's strength, everyone but Zac.

Remaining suspicious, Sarah makes her intentions known but with a warning, "Americans... Another invasion? If this is true, then you will, you must help me. But also, do not underestimate me."

"Sure, O.K." With the gun still pointed at him, Zac gestures submissively as he slowly takes out the picture her parents gave him and extends it to her.

Sarah releases the sailor. He sheepishly walks back and stands next to Major Chapman who quietly comments, "We've really got to work on your skills ol' boy."

Immediately recognizing the photo, Sarah slowly lowers her gun as she walks towards Zac. Her eyes well up. "Follow me."

Nick is amazed as Sarah handily moves a heavy cabinet, revealing a hidden door. He nudges Zac. "Is everybody here as strong as—" Sarah's gaze stops Nick, who nervously smiles back.

Sarah motions. "This way." As Nick walks past the cabinet, he gives it a shove, but it doesn't budge.

Zac quietly asks Nick, "Ever meet a woman stronger than you?"

"*Oh, yeah!*" Nick grins.

With a glance, Sarah admonishes Nick.

"I mean..." Nick sheepishly adds.

Zac just shakes his head.

Sarah leads all down to the infirmary's basement and then through sweltering storm drains to a room sheltering women and their handicapped children. A woman hands her blind one-year-old to Zac. The baby studies Zac's face and laughs.

Zac turns towards Ben, who sternly reminds all, "No! This is not a rescue mission. This could jeopardize everything."

Zac gazes at the playful baby, while reminding Ben, "This...this is what it's all about."

"Zac's right." Jacob is moved by the desperation in the eyes of the women and their children.

"We're not leaving any of them." Nick is adamant.

"Most certainly not!" Jacob shares Nick's sentiment.

"*Hear, hear!*" The Major is quick to add to the consensus.

All stare at Commander Aharon who sees the desperation in their eyes.

Looking at Sarah, Zac smiles and assures her, "We'll think of something." Zac's comment momentarily rescues a callous-sounding Ben from his dilemma as commander. Sarah's smile reveals more than just appreciation.

Heading back, Sarah takes the lead. As she guides them, all are amazed at the maze of ventilation ducts taking advantage of the geothermal region the city is built on. Fortunately, the ducts are large enough to allow them to comfortably walk through.

Lively conversation lures Zac towards a wall vent where he overhears officers discussing a banquet planned for that night. All slow, but Zac motions them on.

Sarah remains behind with Zac who ponders, "Do you think—"

"*I do*, and yes, I can get you in," Sarah is surprisingly quick with her own sarcasm. She smiles and sashays away as Zac, somewhat smitten, finds himself swallowing hard.

CHAPTER 20

❖

Back on the surface, they catch up to Jacob. Fascinated by his surroundings, his meandering has caused him to lag far behind the others.

As they walk, Sarah notices Zac spying a distant cavernous opening. "No. You must not even think of going there."

"Why, where does it lead?"

Sarah calmly delivers a profound revelation, "To the land beyond the poles."

Zac quickly stops, his mind racing. "Beyond the Poles?"

Jacob shakes his head. "*I don't believe it!*"

"A hollow earth?" Zac can barely get the words out.

An amused Sarah looks at Jacob then at Zac. "That's what some call it."

"*I don't believe it!*" Jacob reiterates.

Seeing Zac becoming anxious at the prospect of such a monumental discovery, Sarah becomes emphatic in her warning, "*Please*, some things should be left alone!"

Zac defends his enthusiasm, "The archeological find of all times and you're telling me no?"

"*I—*" Jacob starts.

"*Don't!*" Zac warns.

"Believe it." Sarah assures.

Jacob chuckles and gestures his concession. Sarah takes a deep breath as she anticipates a barrage of questions. She finds a place to sit. With all that has transpired and now this startling discovery, Zac has become fascinated with Sarah and perhaps a bit enamored.

Zac is about to speak when she suddenly begins her story, "Soon after arriving, people began disappearing. Those found were drained of blood and mutilated."

Jacob and Zac look at each other. Captivated, Zac can barely get the words out, "You're saying these mystical people of legend are blood sucking vampires?"

Sarah stares straight ahead as she remembers. "What we know, what anybody knows about them comes mostly from the occult. Many people, not just Nazis, have embraced these creatures and their fables."

"To be sure!" Jacob is quick to chime in.

Zac remains focused on Sarah's previous revelation, "The opportunity of a lifetime!" He anxiously paces. "To finally get to the truth!"

Jacob sighs, expressing his frustration, "Zac, you can report the facts 'til kingdom come, but people will invariably pick and choose what they want to believe, despite the consequences."

Zac hears the defeat in Jacob's weary voice. "Hey, I'm the cynical one in the family. What's the matter?"

Jacob shrugs. "Just tired. Maybe it's finally time to call it a day."

Zac remains focused. "This is too big! Just one more..." Jacob laughs half-heartedly. "Zac, always one more. Sarah, can you talk some sense into him?"

"Like that could ever happen!" Zac is a little too quick with his response.

Sarah continues, "The Nazis were drawn here, by occult messages, to these beings from beyond the poles. It was soon suspected that these creatures may have been responsible for destroying the Aryan race. So, the Nazis tried to destroy them by using a man-made virus."

"Man-made?" Zac is taken aback.

Sarah nods. "From experiments during the war." She looks on in bewilderment, at Zac and Jacob's stunned demeanor. "When the allies dismantled Germany's pharmaceutical cartels, they found many biological anomalies. An evil all its own was the ethical dilemma wrought by such medical atrocities."

Sarah stops, seeing Zac and Jacob look at each other than at her. Continuing, she adds, "Hitler was just the muscle behind... Please tell me you knew this! Your Nuremberg trials condemned the executives of these cartels, but then your so-called cold war came. Your fears saw to the release of these executives in the hopes of making post-war Germany a powerful ally! We never learn, do we."

"*We?*" An indignant Jacob protests.

Zac's mind races as Sarah turns to challenge Jacob, "Did you think the war was just about fighting swastika's and panzers? No, you fought an ideology rooted in your own back yard! Why did you release them? The Nazis were shocked at their good fortune and of the world's short memory. They knew the moment to strike had come. The saboteurs were selected. A time-line was set."

Jacob is overwhelmed and looks for support. "Zac?"

"Later." Zac's mind is racing. "Right now, I just want to know how you delivered a virus?"

Sarah feels a burden being lifted as she shares her story.

"The Nazis had long been trading blood for technology." With a troubled gaze, she continues, "They simply contaminated the blood."

Zac looks at Jacob. "There's your answer to all that blood production."

"Jumpin' Jenner's Jesuits!" Jacob rants, "With the slow infusion of these saboteurs, not to mention those we greedily smuggled in, and with this new technology, the Nazis could win. They could launch an unbeatable, covert counterattack, from within our own borders, both politically and *medically*! And we may have pushed their timetable way up with the release of those flying disks."

"We've still got the element of surprise." Zac states.

"And little else." Jacob laments.

Zac turns to Sarah. "What happened with the virus?"

"Yes, why aren't they all dead?" Jacob's curiosity is as peaked as Zac's.

"They died..." Sarah hesitates. "But soon there were more disembodied spirits than bodies left to inhabit. For lack of a better term, they became legions before our eyes."

"That's some side effect." Zac comments.

A chill comes over Sarah as she exposes the most terrifying of discoveries, "Autopsies revealed their tissue is comprised of sulphur, carbon, hydrogen, nitrogen and oxygen."

"But that's—" Jacob starts.

"Yes, ectoplasm, the stuff of ghosts and demons." Sarah concurs.

Zac looks at Sarah in disbelief. "You're not saying—"

"I'm saying don't go there." Sarah staunchly reiterates.

This discovery gives an already apprehensive Jacob, pause. "Zac, maybe this is one time, I mean, not all things are good or even possible for us to know."

Sarah presses on with an intriguing revelation, "Many of them also possessed a very high somatid content."

"English, please." A puzzled Zac wryly queries.

Jacob, being well-versed in somatids, offers an explain, "Somatid: from the Greek word *soma* meaning *the body* and *tidos* meaning *he who creates*. Also known as microzymas.

Robert T. Estorga

Almost indestructible, these somatids are abundant in our own blood. They help keep life in perpetuation by condensing, by manifesting energy. They were found while attempting to analyze the blood found on the Ark."

"You added these somatids?" Zac is confused.

"No! They were still in the blood!" Jacob excitedly states.

Zac turns to Sarah. "You're saying these beings are crazy for these 'essence of life' somatids?"

"To them, somatids are essentially proof-of-life. They are as mad for somatids as the Nazis are for acquiring their advanced technology."

Jacob questions, "But if they have no blood, no supply, where'd they get somatids before?

A wind whips up as Zac realizes the answer. "Abductions."

Sarah continues, "They've been among us for centuries, perhaps longer. Experimenting, not just to understand us, but to become alive, like us."

Jacob ponders. "Considering the tales of horror found suppressed in some abductees, I'm surprised nobody put this together sooner. Folklore still portrays them as benevolent, wise creatures."

Zac can only draw a terrifying conclusion, "So, blood sucking vampires."

Sarah garners an even more terrifying hypothesis, "Essentially, and now infected, they pose an unimaginable threat to the world. They seem to hate us as much as they need us. Almost as if they were jealous of us."

"Envy has always had more in common with hatred than admiration." Jacob states.

Sarah finally adds, "The fact that ectoplasm deteriorates in light has made it easy to control them with a battery of floodlights aimed at the cavern entrance."

"One wonders whether they weren't responsible for all vampire legends," Jacob suggests.

"Isn't Halloween over?" Zac sarcastically remarks.

"Great Saint Martin de Porres!" Jacob exclaims, "That's it!"

"Martin de Porres isn't even a Saint." Zac retorts.

"Beatification is just as good." Jacob defends his statement before explaining, "But Zac, Halloween didn't officially start until midnight, really November 1st! At one time, it was a three-day celebration that always ended with a huge bonfire and blood sacrifices."

"Then our little surprise on the third is right on the mark." Zac surmises. He sees Jacob seemingly distraught. "What is it?"

"They want to re-establish Halloween, blood sacrifices and all, world-wide." Jacob's realization is disturbing.

Zac asserts, "And we've seen to it that the Nazis, along with their ideology, have been firmly entrenched in our fair land, thanks to Operation Paperclip!"

Jacob further laments, "The stage has been set, by our own hands."

"This is bad." Befuddled, Zac rallies the most monumental of understatements.

Troubled by Jacob's frightening conclusion, Sarah offers an ominous caveat, "I pray for your success but remember, this is just one of many entryways throughout the world."

Sensing Sarah's anxiety, Zac touches her shoulder to reassure her. "Don't worry."

Sarah quickly embraces Zac. "Promise you'll take me with you."

Surprised, Zac can only stammer, "Sure."

Quietly sorting through the facts, Jacob poses a shocking deduction, "These creatures and their legions... Entombment, of a sort, without escape, without death as an escape. Perpetual lifelessness without benefit of rejuvenation. It's almost as if these creatures had been—"

"Don't say it!" Zac is quick to caution.

"*Judged!*" Jacob defiantly states his summation.

Zac sighs. "You had to say it."

Jacob shrugs. "It makes sense."

All this talk has made Zac anxious. "We'd better head back."

"There is one more thing." Sarah quietly states.

With all that has been revealed, Jacob looks at Zac. "I'm afraid to ask."

"What is it?" Zac concedes.

Sarah looks away before continuing, "Eventually, the Nazis experimented by combining discarded ectoplasm with somatids. Those who were deemed expendable were injected first. Strength and energy output increased as did a ravenous requirement for all sources of fuel. Sarah pauses. "All but one patient died."

Sarah is visibly upset and slowly walks away. Zac and Jacob follow.

Zac begins to ask, "What did they—?"

"I was the only one to survive!" Sarah interrupts with a shocking revelation.

Her startling confession stops Zac and Jacob in their tracks. She stops and turns, causing Zac and Jacob to take a step back. Sarah laughs.

"Don't worry, I don't bite."

"But you're a fellow doctor." Zac exclaims.

Jacob agrees. "Yes, why would they experiment on you?"

Sarah confesses, "In their eyes, I'm a Jew first. I was expendable. That is, until my blood was thought to have developed a resistance to the virus. They infused a volunteer, a Mr. Beck, with my blood. He then left on assignment. I presume he underwent the same changes."

"Oh, yeah, just one step closer to a master race." It's all making sense to Zac. "This just gets better and better."

As they resume walking, Sarah reaches for Zac's hand.

CHAPTER 21

◆━━━━━━━━━━◆

Sarah has smuggled Zac and Nick into the banquet kitchen area and assigned them to be waiters. As Zac fumble with his apron strings, Sarah assists by reaching from behind. Her touch awakens long forgotten emotions in both.

"Get back, it's Beck!" Seeing Beck approach, Nick hurriedly shuffles Zac and Sarah through some swinging storage doors.

Light from the small storage window outlines Sarah's soft features. Her hands come to rest on Zac's waist as her eyes hold his gaze. They draw close.

Suddenly, the door swings open as Nick's hand grabs Zac's apron strings and pulls him back into the kitchen, leaving Sarah to stand alone in the storage room. Zac turns and moves towards the storage room doors, but an anxious Nick slips past Zac and opens it first.

"C'mon Sarah, the coast is clear."

A jittery Nick whispers while scanning the room, "Something got Beck to leave in a hurry!"

Nick notices Zac is distracted.

"Hey, Zac, c'mon, let's see..." Nick spies Zac smiling at a blushing Sarah who is shyly smiling back. "Uh-huh, okay." Nick resists the urge to tease.

"Okay, what?" Zac gets defensive.

Nick raises his hands. "Sorry for interrupting."

"What? You weren't..." Zac looks at Sarah then back at Nick, "I mean, you could've..."

Nick slaps Zac on the shoulder. "Real smooth, let's go."

Moments after entering the noisy banquet hall, a seated and very drunk female saboteur asks Zac for a drink, in German, "At-vahs tsoo tring-ken."

A quick-thinking Zac raises a cautionary finger. "English?"

The female saboteur, tipsy and amused, salutes Zac. "Ah, yes, English, thank you. You don't look familiar. Where do you come from?"

"The kitchen." Zac forces a smirk.

The female saboteur laughs, "Your comprehension is terrible, but I like that in a man."

The female saboteur puts a cigarette to her mouth, waiting for a light. Zac obliges. As he leans forward, she slips her address into the side pocket of his jacket. Zac leans further forward, appearing to whisper. As he does, he takes the note and slips it into the jacket of a nearby female saboteur.

The saboteur removes her cigarette. Leaning in, she whispers seductively, "I hope you like surprises."

"I hope you do, too." Zac whispers back.

An S.S. officer walks towards the podium, where Zac's table lies, just below the 5-foot-high platform. In anticipation, everybody at the table motions for Zac to fill their wine glasses. Surveying the room, the officer taps his wine glass, then raises his hand for silence. Beck and two guards climb the platform and stand to the side of the S.S. officer. Beck diligently searches the room. Zac quickly turns and backs against the platform, just under Beck.

Without turning, the S.S. officer speaks, "Satisfied?"

Beck reluctantly nods. The S.S. officer, annoyed at the interruption, chides Beck.

"May I?"

Frustrated, Beck abruptly leaves the banquet.

The S.S. officer begins, *"The secret to victory lies in the establishment of the sciences as the only logical moral compass."*

The hall erupts in applause.

"The most important lessons will come by impressing nature's law of indifference towards the periodical cleansing of genetic corruptions, for the sake of a superior environment."

The crowd begins shouting their approval, bringing more applause as the officer raises his hand.

"Then, as planned, science and all ideologies will be made to stumble, to frustrate, paving the way to self-discipline, self-realization...ultimately leaving the ego to nurture one's own indifferences towards suffering."

Above sporadic shouts of support, he shouts. *"Allowing the unthinkable to, once again, become thinkable!"*

Amid spontaneous cheering and chanting, he strategically pauses, allowing the crowd to whip itself into a frenzy. He pounds the podium while stating the unthinkable.

"The extermination of genetically inferior races, the weeds of humanity that are a biological menace to the future of civilization! Heil Hitler!"

The insanity of the moment has some screaming. The S.S. officer plays to the crowd, doubling his fists, he shouts, *"To again realize that charity towards the unfit is a crime of wasted resources."*

The crowd begins to chant, *"Heil Hitler, Heil Hitler, Heil Hitler!"*

Controlling his rage, Zac steps out onto the balcony and looks up at the stars. Sarah watches. Admiring Zac's passion, she follows and cautiously attempts to offers a sympathetic voice, "For too long, I have heard that same speech... I hate it."

Tempering his anger, Zac appears to not hear. Sarah touches his shoulder as she attempts to sooth his turmoil by changing the subject. "Zachary, please... Tell me about your visit to my village."

He turns to find Sarah only inches away. "Most of the time was spent at a nearby castle."

"I know this castle!" Sarah's face lights up. "In the springtime, my family would picnic there and the view, I remember, it was so beautiful, especially the lake." Sarah presses close.

"Please, tell me more."

Zac's awkwardness is obvious. "Really wasn't there very long, but I'll never forget the view."

Sarah looks deep into Zac's eyes. "So...it survived the war?"

Zac hasn't the heart to tell her of the castle's destruction. "It survived, but someone's idea of renovation was a bit, excessive. Nothing a little m—"

Sarah interrupts with a kiss.

Zac smiles.

Sarah reaches for his hand, "That is...mostly a thank you for what you are doing."

"Mostly?"

"Hi, Sarah." The moment is lost as Nick hurries past. "C'mon Zac, we've got to tell the commander about those saboteurs."

Zac turns to Sarah. "I'll be back."

Sarah sighs at yet another interruption.

Hurrying through the storm drains, voices can be heard emanating from a nearby vent. Zac taps Nick's shoulder and motions him over. They fail to see the boots of someone standing near the vent. They marvel at the size and lavishness of the room. Suddenly, a gravelly voice sends chills down their backs. Their jaws suddenly drop at the sight of Hitler, seated near a fireplace, signing papers, and shaking hands with businessmen and assorted dignitaries.

Nick manages to speak first, "He's alive. What do we do?"

"The fools." Zac's anger is obvious.

"We can't blow this place, not with them in it." Nick fears this sudden development could put their plans on hold.

"Ever have to bomb a city?" Zac sees things a little differently.

A somber Nick nods. "Yeah…orders, you know. But that was war—"

"Do you really think that at war's end, a handshake or signing a piece of paper could stop an ideology?" Zac's rage wells up.

Nick's war memories, long suppressed, are rekindle along with a bitter remorsefulness. "Lighting up a city…" Nick pauses.

Zac quietly remark, "I guess there are times when nobody's innocent."

The radio squawks, and everyone is escorted out. Hitler waits as the room slowly empties.

"Margaret, good to hear from you. Ha! Nobody's called me by that name in a long time. Congratulations on your position… Yes, just finished… All is going as planned."

"Let's go." Nick grows impatient.

Zac has other plans. "I'm going to see what Sarah knows."

"Don't take long." Nick cautions.

As Zac climbs the stairs of the balcony, he hears Sarah's cry for help. Rushing up the stairs, he sees Sarah struggling with a Nazi officer. Zac charges.

"Who was that man? What were you talking about?" The Nazi demands answers.

Zac grabs and spins the officer around. "Why don't you ask me?"

Zac swings at the officer who easily catches Zac's fist before it lands. Zac realizes the Nazi, like Beck, has superhuman strength. A quick-thinking Zac knees him hard in the groin. The officer grimaces, then buckles over.

Turning towards Sarah, Zac remarks, *"Glad some things still work."*

Sarah's stunned look causes Zac to quickly turn. The Nazi has risen and slowly draws his gun. Zac charges and wrestles for the gun, forcing it against the Nazi's chest and his own. It discharges. A tense moment later, the officer falls dead. His eyes suddenly transform into a reptilian shape, revealing a terrifying secret.

"No!" Sarah exclaims, "What have they done?"

Zac stands in disbelief. "Tell me I'm seeing things."

Sarah comes to a terrifying realization. "The saboteurs, they're all…" Sarah's words trail as she looks on in horror. Behind Zac, a spirit rises from the Nazi's body. *"Zac!"* She cries out.

Zac turns just as the spirit plunges into his body. Just as quickly, the spirit appears driven out, screeching as it disappears into the night. In pain, Zac grabs his side and wound.

Grimacing, Zac forces a smile. *"I guess…two's a crowd."*

Sarah stares in astonishment at Zac's wound then quickly embraces him.

"This is too much!"

Zac recovers. "You're not kidding. I've got to warn the others. Pack your things—"

Sarah quickly steals a kiss.

Zac holds Sarah close. "I'll come back for you… I promise." Making his way through the dark passageway, he realizes that Sarah is slowly occupying his thoughts and filling a forgotten void. Smiling as he rounds a corner, he is struck hard. Before blacking out, Zac glimpses Beck emerging from shadows.

CHAPTER 22

◆

D AZED AND DISORIENTED, Zac squints, bringing a hovering
Beck into focus. In a rage, Zac lunges at him but is
stopped by restraints. He fully awakens to find himself
handcuffed to an autopsy table and an I.V. protruding from
his arm.

"Doctor Gomes." Beck grins. "I thought I killed you...
No matter. To the point, I need to know how you got here
and what you are up to?"

"I've got nothing to say to you." Zac speaks with
contempt as he struggles.

"But of course." Beck strolls past Zac. "Your tenacity
is legend. However, though I appreciate a good adversary,
enough is enough. I'm sure, even you tire of the chase." Beck
smiles, "I'd like you to meet a mutual acquaintance."

He turns toward an adjacent autopsy table as something
struggles under the covers. Beck pulls the sheet back,
revealing a distraught Sarah. He strokes Sarah's hair,
relishing the moment.

"I had thought we might become friends. As you
probably know, Sarah and I went through the same, shall
we say, genetic improvements, hence the shackles. Isn't that
right, my dear?"

Beck leans down and removes the gag from Sarah's mouth.

A teary-eyed Sarah looks at Zac who now pleads with Beck, "Let her go, she's innocent."

Beck raises his head. "What was that you said? Ah, yes, *sometimes, nobody's innocent.*"

"I'm so sorry." Sarah tearfully begs Zac's forgiveness.

"Very touching." A heartless Beck reveals their fate, "Let me explain how this works. You and our precious Sarah are attached to a very efficient pump. The lever between you determines the direction of blood flow. One of you will engorge with blood as the other grows painfully cold. One will die an agonizing death, while the other, a slightly less agonizing death. What a rare opportunity to test newfound affections."

Beck's demeanor turns cold as he connects the last switch. Suddenly seeming amused, he chatters, "Can't decide? In fifteen seconds, the pump will decide for you."

Turning away, Beck adjusts a dial as the pump builds pressure. Zac strains to grab the lever, attempting to turn it towards himself. A weakening Sarah reaches out and gently puts her hand over his and softly smile.

"Forgive me." She seizes the lever and throws it in Zac's direction before snapping it off. Zac is overwhelmed with pain while Sarah struggles with her shackles.

Beck is intrigued by Sarah's decision and turns away to check the pump. "Honestly, Dr. Gomes, I'm just as surprised as you. I thought she was beginning to like you. For heaven's sake Sarah, stop struggling before you hurt—

Beck frantically shuts down the pump. He reaches for Sarah's arm and turns it, revealing a torn, mangled wrist and watches as her blood pulses down the drain. Sarah lies motionless.

As Beck tries to stop the bleeding, Zac sits up with a startling realization, he has Sarah's strength. He snaps his handcuffs, seizes Beck by the neck and throws him against the wall. Beck quickly recovers and retaliates.

Zac attempts to fight but struggles with landing punches.

Beck snidely remarks, "Does take some getting used to."

Still the stronger, Beck finally shoves an exhausted Zac against the wall and draws his gun. He smiles as he slowly takes aim. Suddenly the door violently slams open.

Before Beck can react, Nick shoots the gun from his hand, then smiles as he puts his gun down and his fists up.

"I got this one."

"Nick, no!" Zac staggers forward to help just when Beck hits Nick, sending him flying backwards and into Zac. Both career into the cabinets.

Zac can't resist. "Still think it was a lucky punch?"

Nick shakes off the hit and rushes Beck. Despite injuring Beck's hand, it is a vicious fight as Nick exchanges blow for blow with Beck who is relentless. Nick reels with every savage blow but Beck is no fighter and leaves himself open as Nick delivers a flurry of knock-out punches. Finally, an exhausted Nick stumbles back against the cabinets next to Zac. Exhausted and bloodied, Beck retrieves his gun and takes aim.

Sensing someone, Beck turns to see Ben standing in the doorway, pointing a sawed-off, double-barreled shotgun.

Ben smiles. "Knock, knock."

Beck sneers, then whips his gun towards a steely-eyed Ben who fires both barrels. The blast rips into Beck's chest, slamming him against the wall. Zac quickly snatches Nick's gun and points it at Beck.

Nick stands puzzled. "Zac, he's dead!"

"Maybe, maybe not."

"Sarah!" Ben exclaims.

Zac rushes to Sarah's side.

Working frantically, Ben starts a saline solution through her I.V., but it is too late. Zac stares in disbelief.

"Sorry, Zac. We got here as fast as we could." Nick attempts to console Zac.

Pained but composed, Zac becomes resolute. "We're taking her with us."

CHAPTER 23

A MOURNFUL ZAC CARRIES Sarah's draped body. Approaching U-234, spy that the Nazi platoon has returned. The Nazi captain motions for two crewmen from a neighboring U-boat to assist as they board U-234. The four nervous crewmen on U-234's deck stand silent and helplessly outnumbered.

Zac gently lays Sarah's body down, behind some crates. From their vantage, our trio watches.

"Where is your commander?" The Nazi captain's abruptness startles the crew. "Where are your work orders?" In disguise, Major Chapman and three crewmen approach from another U-boat but do not arouse suspicion.

While mulling the best course of action, Zac picks a straw from a crate and sticks it in his mouth.

Nick anxiously looks around and picks up a small ax. "C'mon, I'm rustin' here."

"Hang on, I'm thinkin'." Zac's mind races.

Three passing Nazi crewmen have managed to sneak up and crouch atop the crates and behind our trio. As Ben leans back, he looks up at a squatting Nazi, smiling broadly. Ben nervously taps the others who look back, then at each other. They yank the Nazis down and swiftly engage in a muffled brawl. Major Chapman spies the scuffle and gestures the others to be ready. Zac suddenly lifts one Nazi and with a mighty heave, sends him soaring. He lands with a thud on U-234's deck.

Startled, the Nazi captain and the others gaze at the downed Nazi, then towards Zac, who stands defiant. Bloodied, he glares vengefully at the Nazi captain. Major Chapman and the crew seize the moment and attack. Major Chapman smiles as the sailor who first confronted the Major, now fights with great effect. Nick and Ben charge ahead.

Zac, now filled with an unforgiving resolve, outruns them and slams into the melee, delivering bone-crushing blow after blow. One Nazi stumbles back from a savage hit by Zac and knocks the shortest Nazi down an open hatch.

Enraged, Zac pins the last Nazi against the subs conning tower and beats him until his bloodied fist is heard pounding against metal. Major Chapman and the others struggle to restrain him by pinning him against the conning tower.

Thoroughly exhausted, Zac utters, "I'm so...hungry."

The crewmen release Zac and begin congratulating each other on their victory. They grow silent as Ben approaches, followed by Nick, now carrying Sarah's draped body. With great care, they lower and securely place Sarah's body next to the Ark.

CHAPTER 24

B ELOW DECK, BEN sits, waiting for a report from Zac who enters, resolute and focused. "Commander, they plan to launch a fleet of U-boats loaded with saboteurs."

"Perfect, thank you." Ben is grateful for the report but more concerned for Zac's state of mind. He attempts to console Zac, "You know, sometimes things happen for a reason."

Seeing Nick and Jacob approaching, Ben reveals some of his plan, "My crew has commandeered a U-boat and boarded the women and children. Leaving last, they'll set course for the Falklands. You three, Ensign Casey and I will man U-234."

"*Unbelievable!*" Zac erupts. "*Why not!* I'm sure you've included some vague chance of survival. What are the odds? Assuming there are odds left?"

"Odds are a funny thing." Under the circumstances, Ben ignores Zac's borderline insubordination.

"Sir, Zac and the Professor are civilians." Nick reminds Ben.

"*Haven't you heard? There's a new war in town.*" Ben's mood suddenly changes. He pauses. "Until we're free of twisted ideologies, the luxury of innocence doesn't exist."

Zac begins to regret his —*nobody's innocent*— comment.

"Nonsense, we have a boat full of the innocent…and a responsibility—"

"*Enough!*" Ben loudly interrupts. "I don't suppose you got a departure time for those saboteurs?" Regaining his composure, Ben looks at Zac, then Nick before continuing, "We must do everything we can to insure a successful escape for the others."

"About the saboteurs…" Zac wavers. "There not exactly… human."

"*I knew it!*" Jacob states emphatically.

Ben is at a loss for words and shrugs. "Alright, I'm game. What are they?" He looks at Jacob then back at Zac. "What, exactly, does this mean?"

Before Zac can answer, Jacob exclaims, "It means that the saboteurs are the biggest threat to mankind since—" Jacob hesitates, catching a glimpse of Zac's exasperation at the notion of what Jacob is about to infer, "Since the fall!"

"Those flying discs…" Nick jumps in. "We could've pushed their timetable way up. We have to act fast!"

"*Yes!*" Ben is quick to agree. "Ensign, advise the others to be ready to launch."

"Aye, sir." Ensign Casey hurries off to relay the command.

Ben turns to Nick. "Can the bomb be detonated from here?"

Nick swallows hard before delivering the bad news, "No, but the timer can be manually turned to cause instant detonation. Whoever goes…isn't coming back."

"*I'll do it,*" Zac quickly volunteers.

"*Nonsense, they won't suspect me!*" Jacob contests.

Nick's bravado emerges as he taps his chest. "*Hold on.* I have the best chance."

Zac begins to argue, "*Now look—*"

Jacob quickly tries reasoning, "*But in an officers' uniform, they won't suspect—*"

"I'm going and that's that." Zac states forcefully.

As they continue to argue, a waist-high stream of water appears, catching everyone's attention. Ben has punctured his hot water bottle and squeezed out its contents. As the stream dissipates, a flatulent sound emerges.

Ben takes charge. "To assure success, Nick and Zac will both have to try."

Jacob agrees, almost, "Ben's right, uh, what about me?"

"Sorry, Jacob, but I need you here."

Ensign Casey hands flashlights to Nick and Zac as Ben explains, "I have a back-up plan."

Ben's sudden comment sets an unsettling tone with Zac and Nick.

"But I need their departure time. Signal me the time and if you fail, we'll still have a chance at stopping them."

As Ben steps away to check dials, Nick whispers to Zac, "Do you think Ben's ever been...you know, tested?"

Jacob murmurs a famous line he'd once read, "Ours is not to wonder why..."

"Ours is but to do—" Zac quietly attempts to finish.

"Or die." Nick interrupts.

"No, it's *and* die." Zac corrects him.

"I like...*or* die." Nick sees things differently and speaks up, "Why does it have to be...*and* die?"

"Because it is!" Zac loudly retorts.

As they banter, Ben strolls by and stops. He talks without addressing anyone, "I'm starting a new book... The Alamo."

"That's not funny!" Zac grumbles.

Ben reiterates, "Get me that departure time!"

As Zac and Nick prepare to leave, noises from above draw them to the observation window. Shocked by what they see, they climb and cautiously peer from atop U-234's conning tower. Both are shaken at the sight of an impromptu sendoff on the U-boat dock.

"To our magnificent Ambassadors, twelve hundred strong, success and victory...Heil Hitler!" The S.S. officer from the banquet rouses the crowd as the saboteurs march their way onto the U-boats.

In unison, the saboteurs chant, *"Heil Hitler!"*

Zac leans back. "We're too late."

"No..." Nick turns away and soberly contemplates what he's about to say, "I can detonate the other bomb right here, right now."

"I've made my peace." That suits Zac just fine.

Nick hesitates. "The others..."

"These monsters can't be allowed to leave," Zac rationalizes as he lets his frustrations dictate the fate of the others, "We all knew this could happen." Zac turns as if to observe the saboteurs. "Make it fast."

One by one, the 30 U-boats slowly begin to back away, submerging as they go.

Nick and Zac hurry back down. Before he rushes off, Nick extends his hand to Zac. "Sorry for getting you and Jacob into this mess."

Jacob walks in. "What's going on?"

He can hear the clamor coming from outside, but Zac's silence says it all.

"They're leaving now, aren't they?"

Jacob's fears are confirmed by Nick's hasty departure towards the torpedo room.

A perceptive Jacob resigns to their fate. "And Nick... Good, I hate long good-byes."

"Sorry." Moments away from obliteration and Zac can only muster a simple apology.

"Nonsense!" Jacob is more poignant. "I'm with you...and that's everything. Well, one more piece of my Aunt's carrot cake would hit the spot right about now."

Ben enters and is surprised to see Zac. Before he can speak, Zac reports, "There leaving, now."

Ben grabs the intercom and gives the command, "Ensign, prepare to get underway! Notify the others!" Looking around, he asks, "Where's Nick?"

"Torpedo room." Zac calmly replies.

Ben orders the Ensign, "Keep your distance from those U-boats." Turning, he politely addresses Jacob, "Professor, to your station!"

With the imminence of death looming, Zac exclaims, *"Station... Now?"*

Jacob is suddenly inspired by a line from an old poem, *"Because I could not stop for death — Death kindly stopped for me."* Zac extends his hand, but Jacob bear hugs him as he explains, "Duty's last call. Better than standing around."

As Jacob begins to leave, Ben gestures to Zac, "Care to join me?"

Zac looks back at Jacob who chuckles. "I guess there'll be no avoiding this family reunion."

CHAPTER 25

U-234 MANEUVERS BEHIND the last departing U-boat. From behind U-234, the commandeered U-boat, now housing rescued women and children, quickly sets course for the Falklands. The damaged U-234 struggles to keep up with the U-boat pack.

Ensign Casey reports, "Sir, we're losing ground."

The strain of waiting for the inevitable is too much for Zac. He utters under his breath, *"C'mon, Nick, what's taking so long?"* His inpatients' gets the best of him. "Can't this thing go any faster?"

Ben is amused. "Something wrong, Dr. Gomes?"

"We can't let any of them escape!"

Nick quickly rushes in and confronts Ben. "Uh, commander, where's the bomb?"

"Where is it?" Zac is stunned.

The Ensign breaks into the conversation to report, "Sir, we are at maximum speed and falling behind..."

Ben remains silent.

"Sir?" Ensign Casey's tone makes known his concern.

"You knew this was going to happen!" Zac snaps.

Nick paces, frustrated, he suddenly leans into Ben and speaks with intensity, *"Excuse me... The bomb?"*

Finally, Ben motions all to follow him. As they enter U-234's cargo hold, Zac sees the Ark strapped onto a lifeboat.

The sight of Sarah's draped body next to the Ark is too much for Zac. *"First Mike, now Sarah. Why...Why not me?"* A question that will forever haunt him.

Ben uncovers and slaps a one-man mini-sub. "I was beginning to think we wouldn't be able to execute my plan. By the way, whose idea was it to blow us all up?"

Nick and Zac look at each other.

"Too bad, good plan. Anyway, the new plan is for me to get in fast and close using the mini-sub. I'll be utilizing the starboard torpedo's engine to boost my attack speed. At a thousand feet out, I will fire the portside torpedo, now loaded with the other bomb. By then, U-234 should be backing away at full speed." Ben gestures towards the starboard torpedo. "I managed to remove the detonator, just wish there'd been time to remove the charge. Would've given me more—"

"That's too close." Zac has heard enough. "We'll be a thousand feet from you, and you, what, a thousand feet from them, at best? You planned this to be a one-way trip, for all of us!"

"There must be another way?" Nick stands in agreement.

"No time!" Ben remains steadfast. "This is it!" He challenges Zac. "You asked me earlier about our odds. Were you talking the mission or your own survival?"

Zac calms down and attempts reasoning, "Look, couldn't we—?"

"The ship is damaged." Ben loses his patients. *"With every second we lose ground. I will be firing as close to them and as quickly as I can. By then, you should be safely underway. My fate will be in my hands!"*

All are taken aback by the Ben's outburst. Nick suddenly remembers a promise he made to a young Airman and pulls out Mike's letter, but Zac approaches Ben first. He pulls out and offers Mike's prayer book and Yamaka to Ben. "Maybe this… It belonged to a very brave young man."

Ben recognizes and snatches the frayed book and Yamaka from Zac who suddenly realizes he has unwittingly and callously delivered devastating news.

Nick's eyes widen as he rushes to Ben's side and hands him Mike's letter. "*Ben*, I'm sorry."

Momentarily overwhelmed, a tortured Ben slowly raises his hand. Nick tries to apologize and explain, "I should've told you sooner. Zac didn't know."

Ben slowly looks at Nick, then upwards and closes his eyes, "No, too late… Ensign!"

"Sir!" Ensign Casey displays his readiness.

Squaring his shoulders, Ben turns to face his long-time friend. With devotion stemming from years of service, the Ensign adds a salute, "Yes, sir!" The Ensign then steps back and addresses Nick and Zac, "The Professor is already back in the engine room, ready to reverse engines on my command. Nick, you'll help with steering. Zac, you man the observation window and report everything you see."

As Nick and Zac look on, Ben writes 'Shalom Zachar' on the mini-sub.

The puzzled look on Nick's face prompts Zac to explain, "'*Shalom Zachar*'…*means, in remembrance.*"

Ben writes on the torpedo housing the nuclear bomb, NEVER AGAIN, then looks at Zac. "My Kaddish, what do you think?"

Zac offers an understanding nod and smile.

Nick leans towards Zac. "And, Kaddish?"

Zac quietly explains, "At some point, it's a mourner's duty to rise above personal pain and join others in a common venture. Supposed to make things right between the three of them." Nick's perplexed look earns him an explanation with a dose of sarcasm. "The departed, the mourner and Yahweh... Thought you were with intelligence?"

Nick returns the sarcasm, "Sorry, keeping up with the Gomeses was never at the top of my list."

Ben has a request of Nick, "Captain, before you go, I'd like you to attach this wire-guided system and bypass the timer on our package."

Admiring Ben's courage, Nick respectfully obliges. "Yes, sir!"

Zac and Ensign Casey proceed to their assignments. Passing the radio room, the Ensign immediately spots the radio powered up and several displaced items. He draws his gun and motions Zac to follow. As Casey eases passed a doorway, a Nazi — *the one that fell down the hatch* — unwittingly steps out between the ensign and Zac. Before he can aim his gun at Casey, Zac spins the Nazi and delivers a crushing blow, snapping his neck. Stunned, Ensign Casey follows as he watches an embittered Zac drag the small-framed body into the torpedo room and stuff it into a torpedo tube.

"But the torpedo tubes are crushed, *only inches*—" Zac's glare says it all. The ensign shuts up. Zac pulls an apple from his pocket and takes a bite as he slaps the control, jettisoning the body. The pressure mangles the Nazi's body as it squirts out.

Back in the cargo bay, Ben struggles with his headphones before testing them, "Ensign, talk to me."

The ensign quickly dons headphones. "Sir, there was a Nazi stowaway. He's dead but he may have radioed our position!" Ben is busy adjusting his headphones and doesn't hear the ensigns warning. Casey assumes that Ben's failed response is due to his contemplative assessment of the situation.

Ben suddenly barks orders, "Flood the cargo bay, open bay doors, prepare to launch!"

"Yes, sir... Godspeed, sir." Removing his headphones, Ensign Casey motions Zac to follow.

As they arrive at U-234's window, Zac dons his headphones and takes his position.

"Zac, talk to me, what do you see?" Casey tests communications.

Zac peers out the window to a surprisingly clear ocean view. "U-boats barely in sight."

As the cargo bay fills, Ben catches a flash out of the corner of his eye. He looks out the mini-sub's window, but sees nothing. He shrugs and disregards as the bay continues to fill. Finally, the cargo doors open, and the mini-sub launches. Unnoticed and just before the doors close, the Ark, strapped to the inflated lifeboat, rises out of the cargo bay. As planned, U-234 navigates to within feet of a huge rock formation at the edge of a deep underwater canyon and waits.

Ben engages the starboard torpedo's motor and throttles up the mini-sub. The added thrust drives Ben back against his seat. Adjusting course, he is surprised to see that all U-boats have stopped. Six of them block his path. Poised in a row and about five hundred yards out, the two outside U-boats fire wire-guided mini-torpedoes.

Ben tenses as he murmurs, *"No, I'm too far!"* He thinks hard and fast as the torpedoes converge on their target. He quickly throws the mini-sub into reverse, attempting to buy time and draw the speeding torpedoes closer to each other as they approach. The starboard torpedo strains against the counteractions of the mini-sub's engine. 60 yards...50 yards, Ben waits, 40 yards...he releases the starboard torpedo at point-blank range. It strikes the farthest torpedo producing an immense blast that sends the second mini-torpedo pitching to within feet of Ben.

It detonates, sending shrapnel into the mini-sub and exploding an oxygen tank, mortally wounding Ben. Cheers goes up as the U-boat crews hear multiple explosions. The mini-sub begins to flood. The U-boats take no chances as four more mini-torpedoes are fired.

Zac is turning to relay the blast when Nick rushes up to Zac's position.

"What was—" Nick freezes as his jaw drops. The sub is suddenly bumped hard. He stands transfixed on the observation window. Zac sees Nick staring and slowly turns to find a whale's eye looking through the window, first at Zac then at Nick. The weight and pressure exerted by the great whale put an audible strain on U-234's hull. Zac touches the window and the whale blinks.

Awed, Zac can only muster, "Great Saint—"

"*Neptune?*" Nick blurts a guess.

"Oh, you'll burn for that one." Zac remarks.

The whale pushes off, knocking Zac and Nick to the deck floor. Leaks spring everywhere. Zac rises to see the whale speed towards the mini-sub.

Casey charges in. "*What was that? Get those leaks! Hurry!*"

In the engine room, the bump from the whale has knocked Jacob unconscious.

The whale charges the mini-sub from behind as the mini-torpedoes converge on their target. As Zac struggles with the leaks at his station, he sees the deadly race and hurries to relay his concern through the intercom, "Uh, the commander's in real trouble, we've got to help him."

"*Stand fast!*" The ensign's own struggle to restore the integrity of U-234 brings a swift response, "The commander is on his own!"

The speeding whale opens his jaws and slowly clamps down on the mini-sub, causing it to partially crumple.

Ben is jarred by the sudden acceleration and exclaims as he sees the whale's teeth close, *"Great Jonah!"*

From U-234's observation window, Zac stares in disbelief. With a mighty surge, the whale charges the U-boats, dodging the torpedoes as they are turned in pursuit. One strikes a glancing blow from behind, exploding on impact, wounding the vengeful whale. Streaming blood, the whale swiftly maneuvers past the six U-boats, making aiming difficult. The whale's wake sends one mini-torpedo into the conning tower of a U-boat. The blast sends the tower violently spinning away, spewing flailing crewmen and debris along its wake. The freezing water rushes in to claim the doomed vessel and remaining crew. The blast has also cut the guide-wire of another mini-torpedo, leaving it to the whim of the current. The last torpedo strikes deep into the whale and explodes. Tons of blubber protect the mini-sub from the shockwave that ripples through the great white whale. The U-boat crews again cheer.

The dying whale's mouth opens and the crumpled minisub shoots out. With gases escaping, it drifts to a stop amidst the fleet of U-boats. Zac has seen it all.

"The commander's one lucky—" Zac stops at the chilling sound of Ben laughing. Staring at the damaged mini-sub, Zac mumbles, *"I've got a bad feeling about this."* He anxiously reports. "Casey, I suggest reversing, now!"

The ensign senses the urgency in Zac's voice and shouts, *"Reverse!* Professor, reverse now... *Jacob!"* Sensing something is terribly wrong, the ensign races to the engine room.

In the mini-sub, the atmosphere is stifling. The control panel smokes and sparks as an oxygen-deprived Ben chuckles. He suddenly becomes quiet. Sweating profusely, Ben slowly lowers his head and closes his eyes. Clutching his son's letter, he smiles. Suddenly, with fervent resolve, he grabs his wound and opens a channel, "To the commander of the U-boats."

The Nazi commander gestures for silence from an anxious crew. Drenched in sweat, he responds, as all U-boats listen in, "Such a brave soul. An admirable performance." The U-boat commander signals to ram Ben's mini-sub. "Now, let us help you." The U-boat slowly turns towards Ben and picks up speed.

As Ben dons his son's Yamaka, he offers the Nazi commander a deadly riddle, "Daphaq-daphaq!" (*Hebrew for Knock-Knock.*)

After hearing Ben's puzzling riddle, Zac makes an anxious query, "Jacob, what does "Daphaq-daphaq" mean...? Jacob!"

In the engine room, the ensign steadies Jacob who, upon hearing Zac's request, lunges at the controls, throwing the engines into reverse. U-234's sudden surge causes Nick to be thrown forward. Instinctively reaching to stop his fall, he grabs the dive controls, causing U-234 to drag the ocean floor stern first. Hitting bottom sends Zac tumbling across the floor. Barely able to rise, he struggles against U-234's violent surge as it drags and bumps along the sea floor. U-234 scrapes a nearby rock formation, knocking a massive boulder onto the forward deck. Their escape is brought to a crawl only feet from an underwater canyon and safety.

Exasperated, Nick shouts, "*Now what*, why aren't we moving?"

Zac rushes to the observation window and sees the massive boulder on U-234's crumpled deck. In the distance, he sees the U-boat closing in on Ben.

"C'mon Ben, light 'em up!"

All have heard Ben's enigmatic message. Many U-boat commanders break their silence and fill the airwaves with anxious, ship to ship, chatter. An S.S. officer grabs the microphone and shouts, *"Silence!"*

Everyone heeds the warning. The stagnant air draws sweat from every pore as all listen intently. The S.S. officer looks around at the terrified crew, then presses the button to respond. Nearby, a sailor whispers into his commander's ear. The commander's eyes widen. He rushes the S.S. officer and yells, *"Nooo!"*

Too late, the arrogant S.S. officer replies in utter contempt, "Who's there?"

Zac suddenly sees the wayward mini-torpedo hurtling directly at U-234. In the distance, he spies the speeding U-boat only feet from striking Ben.

There's an all-encompassing, blinding *FLASH*.

An immense wall of water, violently propelled by the massive shockwave overtakes the wayward torpedo and drives it into the boulder, obliterating it. U-234 is freed, only to be slammed by the massive shock wave. It crushes and mangles the forward compartments. Zac is thrown hard and falls away just as the rolling shock wave strikes the observation window, cracking it with a pop. An unstoppable flood of water surges in. The pressures generated by the nuclear blast quickly drives U-234 back, pitching it down the chasm and to safety. On the fringe of the U-boat pack, a captain looks through his periscope and exclaims the moment before the blast pierces his eyepiece, "So schon hell!" (*German: So beautifully bright!*)

The blast has created a massive event chamber. The whale has vaporized, along with Ben. The diminishing flash reveals U-boats nearest ground-zero have vanished. Others are in a slow downward spin, carrying the hapless crews and saboteurs to a watery grave. Countless white hot, sizzling fragments are streaking in every direction.

In a slow twist, U-234 free-falls stern first. Ensign Casey muscles his way to Nick and Zac. Struggling against the rushing water, he pulls them from the flooding control room. With no time to lose, he returns to close the hatch from inside the control room. Casey is fighting a losing battle when Zac grabs the hatch from the outside and holds it open. He yells above the roar of the rising water, "*Grab my hand!*"

"*Too late!*" To make his point, he aims his sidearm at Zac, who stares in disbelief.

Nick suddenly rushes up and rams his shoulder into the hatch and yells, "*Zac, help!*"

Zac stands in awe at the ensign's resolve to duty. He nods to Casey and with a mighty heave, he and Nick close the hatch. Nick secures it as the ensign shouts through the intercom, "*Abandon ship, secure all hatches along the way!*"

With U-234's bow pointed straight up; they carefully make their way to the cargo hold. A seasick Jacob asks, "Where's Ensign Casey?"

Zac quietly states, "At his post," still in awe of Casey's bravery and sacrifice.

The churning waters push U-234 ever deeper, down the abyss. The sputtering engine finally fails as U-234 silently slips beyond its limits.

U-234 bends and moans as a fearful Jacob asks, "How deep are we?"

Zac comes to a sobering realization, "We've got to blow ballast."

"Control room's flooded," Nick reminds Zac.

As Zac moves towards the hatch. Nick grabs his arm. "*No!* You could flood us with the first hatch you open."

"I'm the only one with a chance." Zac is adamant.

Just then, the ballast blow and all realize it to be the ensign's courageous last act.

"The ensign..." Nick looks at Zac.

"Yeah, like the others." Zac somberly notes.

A bewildered Zac turns to Jacob but before he can speak, Jacob answer, "No, you'd be asking the wrong person."

Everybody feels U-234's rapid ascent. Nick quickly instructs all. "Be ready to move fast, there's no telling how long we'll stay afloat!" Breeching, U-234 juts into the air then gently slips back onto the churning ocean.

Zac forces open the damaged cargo doors and tethers a lifeboat. Countless bits of charred debris, along with tons of catapulted water rain down as each grapple along the rope to safety. The mushroom cloud looms terrifyingly close. All hold fast as Zac cuts the tether moments before a giant wave lifts them away.

CHAPTER 26

Z AC WAKES TO the sound of the surf. The stark sun rouses all to an unbelievable sight. The Ark, still strapped to the lifeboat, rests on the beach. Nick is standing, smiling as he looks out to sea.

Jacob adjusts his glasses and asks, "Are we safe? I suppose that's a rather silly question."

Zac wrestles to his feet and shakes the sand from his hat. Looking over the Ark, he sees a U.S. carrier group next to what's left of U-234. A small launch approaches. Later, after a hot lunch and quick debriefing, Zac, Nick, and Jacob eagerly make their way to the bow of the carrier. Silently hoping against hope, they watch the search and rescue team slowly emerges from U-234. Hearts sink when the lifeless body of Ensign Casey is brought out. Nick and Jacob turn away, but Zac watches as the team secures all hatches, thus ending they're search.

A sailor with his clipboard approaches Zac. "Sir, no other bodies were found." Zac nods.

"Sorry, Zac," Nick slaps Zac's shoulder.

Zac had hoped for Sarah's body to have somehow survived. Looking out to sea, he asks, "It's not over, is it?"

"We can hope." Nick smiles.

"What?" Jacob misunderstands as he tries to clear his waterlogged ears. "Don't give up hope." Zac and Nick just smile.

The captain approaches, but before he can speak, a brilliant flash on the horizon draws their attention. He grumbles, "Not another one."

He quickly eyeballs a guilty-looking trio who pretend to be unaware. He shakes his head and sighs. Turning, he barks orders to the sailor, "Have the search and rescue team ready by 0600."

The sailor snaps to attention. "Yes, sir."

The captain motions all to follow as he shifts his cigar from one side to the other.

"That reminds me!" Zac pulls Abe's cigar from his pocket and tips the dented metal sleeve. Out oozes chocolate. Zac licks his hand.

Nick laughs. "Abe doesn't smoke."

As they walk, Zac spies a helicopter being worked on. "We're gonna need help getting the Ark off this ship."

Nick grins and asks, "Think you can help fly that thing?"

Zac smirks.

CHAPTER 27

━━━━━━━━━━◆━━━━━━━━━━

*T*HE NUCLEAR BLAST *drives a wave of intense heat deep into the surrounding valley's frozen peaks. Tons of mountain snow is driven upwards, where the sub-zero temperatures quickly create an ice storm that pummels the city, already in nightmarish ruins.*

The intense heat also liquifies a nearby glacier, sending tons of raging flood waters and massive boulders slamming into the charred remains of the Third Reich's New Berlin. The blast sends an electronic pulse that cripples scores of escaping disks. Some explode in mid-air, others fall apart as they plummet to the ground, creating a wide debris field.

Within the burning carnage, hordes of raging and disfigured creatures hunt down the remaining Nazis, now running in chaotic desperation.

From within the stalwart Ark, angels swiftly emerge with swords drawn. Some charge the plane carrying the fleeing representatives and quickly surround the fuselage. Those inside are driven to insanity at the sight of the vengeful images. Amid frenzied cries, the plane is violently thrust deep into the forbidden cavern.

A massive windstorm overwhelms the mushroom cloud, carrying it off, while unrelenting hail and ice seal the valley's fate by creating a frozen lake, entombing the city. The wind retreats, as if satisfied, leaving an eerie silence.

A gentle, swirling breeze races across the newly-formed, frozen lake. It seems to stop and dance around the only remaining object, the ARK.

CHAPTER 28

◆————◆————◆

A T PRECISELY 0600, three helicopters carrying search and rescue teams launch. Another helicopter rises but turns in the opposite direction. It slips away, skimming just above the water.

Talking above the rhythmic drone of the helicopter, Nick assures Zac and Jacob, "We should reach the other battle group in an hour. It's too bad about the decoy Ark!"

Zac reminds them, "Was anybody listening when I said you can't destroy the Ark?"

"So, you think it survived?" Nick asks.

"Precisely!" Zac states emphatically.

"Providentially!" Jacob concurs.

Zac offers some cynical assurance. "Don't worry, they'll find a safe place for it!"

Seagulls begin to gather and squawk as they keep pace, surrounding the low flying helicopter. Zac comments, "You know what they say about gathering seagulls?"

"*Whale!*" Jacob shouts.

Zac and Nick turn and loudly agree, "*Right!*"

"*No, WHALE!*" Jacob excitedly points.

Zac and Nick look at each other, then forward to see a breaching white whale moments from impact.

"*WHALE!*" They shout in unison.

Nick pulls up on controls as the whale spins and plunges into the ocean. He remembers Zac's story. "Mocha!"

"He lives on!" Jacob adds.

"Must've been part of that whale's pod." Zac guesses.

"Too bad," Nick states with regret.

"He'll survive." Zac is more optimistic.

Nick looks to his left and mumbles, "*Strange looking fogbank.*"

Jacob speaks up, "You know, something just struck me."

With a bang, a harpoon suddenly slams upwards, piercing the copter's floor, shooting up and through Jacob's leg.

"*AUUGH!*" He writhes in pain as small talons spring open above his leg and another larger set just above the helicopter floor. The harpoon jerks downward with a thud as the larger talons hit the floor first, stopping the upper talons from ripping through Jacob's leg.

While Nick struggles to keep airborne, Zac rushes to unscrew and remove the upper talons. He pulls the steel shaft up through Jacob's bleeding leg and quickly applies a tourniquet.

Despite the pain, Jacob can't help but laugh. "*Ha, 'something just struck me.' Zac...tape my mouth shut too!*"

"Don't tempt me!" Zac jokes, but only to divert Jacob's attention from the pain and severity of his wound.

He returns to help Nick, but despite their efforts, the helicopter begins to be dragged downward. Zac and Nick catch a glimpse of a U-boat, damaged and drifting, stern submerged, at the edge of the fogbank. They also spy two severely burned saboteurs anxiously reeling them closer to the U-boat.

"*The Ark!*" Jacob yells.

"I've got this!" Nick commands, "Zac, take the controls!"

"*No, I'm going to finish this!*"

He looks at Jacob, then at Nick. "Don't wait for me, save the Ark!"

"*Nonsense!*" Jacob voices his objection.

As Zac reaches for the hatch, Jacob puts his hand on Zac's shoulder. Zac hesitates, then leans in close and whispers, "*I remember.*"

Jacob smiles then closes his eyes.

The two saboteurs crouch and watch as Zac climbs out. Using an oily towel, he slides down the harpoon line and onto the deck. His feet strike the deck hard, knocking his gun loose. It falls onto the listing deck and slides down an open hatch. The saboteurs smile and point their guns.

Zac catches a glimpse of something speeding towards the U-boat. Suddenly, the pup whale leaps over the deck. Rolling sideways, it takes out one saboteur with a crunch. The other saboteur watches in horror as both whale and saboteur disappear over the side with a bloody splash.

Turning back, he sees Zac aiming Ben's shotgun. The saboteur quickly raises his gun, but Zac blasts him off the deck.

With every alarm competing for his attention, Nick feels the helicopter slipping from his control. From the corner of his eye, he sees an immense flying disk emerge from the fogbank. It approaches to within feet the helicopter.

A wide-eyed Nick shrinks in his seat and melodically murmurs, "*Zac, hurry it up with that line.*" An electronic signal emanating from the disk causes more fits with the copter's circuitry.

Zac spies the crippled disk menacingly close to the flailing helicopter and rushes to unhook the harpoon line.

He loads another harpoon, aims, and fires. The talons strike deep into the disk, locking onto their prey. Zac watches as the helicopter continues to struggle.

Gazing at the massive disc, then down at the U-boat, Zac knows he must act fast. Reloading the shotgun, he looks up one last time, then jumps down the hatch. From the open hatch, Nick can see the flash of gunfire.

Suddenly, an explosion sends burning fuel through the hatch, igniting the wooden deck. In desperation, Nick and Jacob anxiously watch.

"C'mon Zac." Nick implores.

Jacob closes his eyes. "Dear God, help him."

Tense moments later, a massive blast peels the deck from the hull.

As the burning U-boat sinks, it pulls the disk into the sea. From deep within the huge disk, muffled explosions erupt. Plumes of steam spew while arcs of electricity snap and pop.

Nick quickly pulls away and turns the helicopter. With growing despair, he searches the patches of burning debris for signs of Zac.

CHAPTER 29

———————◆———————

September 23rd, 1979

DAWN'S EARLY LIGHT catches Zac struggling to open a telegram marked URGENT. The sun's rays cause Zac to squint. He turns away, towards the warming fireplace and reads:

Zac, I could get life for this STOP.
One more mission before I retire STOP.
I know this nightclub that just loves to toast STOP.
One more for your Dad, Sarah, and the others STOP.
Stay well STOP.
Keep looking to the horizon STOP.
Nick STOP.

Zac folds the telegram and offers it up to the burning fireplace. 23 years of memories suddenly vie for his attention as he readies himself for yet another celebration. A Chauffeur knocks on the door as he opens it, "Hello, Mr. Gomes? Time to go... Zac?"

Zac nods. Gripping the chair, he rises slowly and grabs a small thermos on his way out.

The limo ride is settling.

The Chauffeur glances back through the rear-view mirror, "I never got a chance to thank you... You know, for your help."

Zac stares out his window, "Don't thank me yet, Danny. Ditch diggin' ain't what it used to be."

"But the exhilaration of discovery must have been rewarding. I mean, for all the time you spent, and the traveling?"

While entertained by the bustle of the city, Zac reflects, "Years, miles, it's a double-edged sword. Just don't lose your own history in the process."

At the bristling new museum, Zac endures a generous hour of fanfare before a solemn moment unveils the final resting place for the Ark of the Covenant. Applause erupts as Zac is again recognized and thanked.

The ride back is quiet.

In front of the Hotel, Zac steps out of the limo, clutching his thermos. He looks up at the Hotel, but turns and walks towards the marketplace. The limo slowly follows Zac as he walks through the unhurried crowds. Stopping to purchase a newspaper, he tucks his thermos and continues. Meandering through the streets, Zac suddenly turns down a long, narrow alley. The limo stops and watches.

Street sounds fade as Zac navigates well-worn steps. Turning again, only his footsteps now break the silence. Coming to a small door, he unlocks it, stoops, and enters. Zac smiles smugly as he sidesteps his way through a bevy of booby-traps, drawn from years of personal experience.

He approaches a carved, wooden door displaying the Taurus constellation on the upper left and a cross on the lower right, signifying the Aleph and the Tav (*Alpha and Omega*). Smiling, he unscrews the bottom of the thermos and retrieves a coin known as the Bull's Eye. Placing it in a depression located in the eye of Taurus, he lets it drop. He listens as it gains speed. Finally tripping a lever, it pops the door open. Entering, he returns the coin to the thermos. There, on a platform made of Meleke limestone — *the stone of kings* —, rests the real Ark of the Covenant. The bond between Zac and the Ark has grown into a lifetime of service.

Zac sets his newspaper on a huge pile of aging newspapers before placing his coffee on a small table. Easing into an old wicker chair, he sips his coffee while pulling a small apple from his coat pocket. He takes a bite. Without looking, he grabs a newspaper and reads the headline:

NASA's FIRST DEEP SPACE PROBE,
PIONEER 10 LAUNCHED - FINAL
DESTINATION: ALDEBARAN SYSTEM.

"*What?*" Zac instantly searches for the date, "1972? Zac, you're losing it."

He tosses the newspaper back onto the pile and grabs another. Before he can unfold it, a familiar pain emanates from his side. Barely able to stand, he clutches his newspaper as he leans against a pillar.

Overwhelming images from his adventures flood his senses. It seems all too real.

A treasure of cherished memories, friendships, then the painful losses and missed opportunities. Suddenly, with hat in hand, he finds himself standing before a grave, and remembers.

A swirling wind quickly descends. Zac dons his hat and looks upwards to see a familiar helicopter struggling to stay airborne. Looking down, he is back on the U-boat as his memories from the battle flood in.

Zac again feels the weight of Ben's shotgun in his hands. Spurred on by the chaotic shouts from below deck, he reloads. He

159

gazes up at the helicopter and is filled with resolve. Braving the pandemonium, he jumps down the hatch. Landing hard, he fires both barrels then picks up his pistol. Outnumbered, he battles thru the U-boat. Driven by a wave of adrenalin from his newfound strength, he fiercely battles his way deep into the U-boat. Turning, he fires his last shot that explodes the ammo in the forward hold (1st blast). Klaxons begin to blare. He is thrown back but is protected from the blast by several crewmen and saboteurs who take the brunt of the flying shrapnel. Zac's fall is stopped by two familiar, angelic figures. The three of them are startled by the sudden presence of a mighty angel wearing blood-stained battle armor and carrying a great sword. Zac sees the two cherubim nod to the angel as if given a command. They quickly envelope Zac with their expanding wings and pass downward, slipping, with ease, through the hull. Zac has the terrifying sensation of drowning as he and the cherubim speed underwater. He is suddenly thrust upwards.

Zac is then given a vision of what happened next in the U-boat.

The charging saboteurs stop and cower at the sight of the angelic warrior standing amidst stacks of torpedoes. He raises his sword. With klaxons blaring, the terrified saboteurs run as the angel strikes (2nd blast).

From the helicopter, Nick looks on in horror as the U-boat explodes. He scans the water, looking for any signs of life…of Zac. In despair, he slumps back in his seat. He is suddenly startled by the sight of Zac sitting next to him, soaking wet and trying to catch his breath. Zac turns to see Jacob who sits motionless. His fears slowly turn to sadness.

Back in the chamber, Zac senses someone behind him. Turning, he sees an apparition wearing a gown commonly worn in ancient times.

The ghostly image begins to take form as it moves towards him. Raising an arm, it reveals a scarred wrist.

Feeling his face being caressed, he winces and closes his eyes. Opening them, he is overwhelmed to see a teary-eyed and ageless... *Sarah*! They swiftly embrace. For Zac, it is soothing and restorative. When they pull away, we see the years have rolled back and Zac is as he was when they first met. Kissing Sarah's scarred wrist, he breathes in a sweet, familiar aroma and smiles.

As they embrace, Zac drops his newspaper. It drifts, landing propped up near the door but hidden in the shadows. There's a flash, then a temblor that knocks the door open. The light illuminates the headline, dated September 1979:

SATELLITE DETECTS NUCLEAR DETONATION NEAR ANTARCTIC – GOVERNMENT DENIES INCIDENT.

CHAPTER 30

Z AC IS GONE, along with Sarah. His beloved hat rests upon the Ark, atop one of the Cherubim.

Suddenly, booby-traps can be heard going off. The entrance becomes strewn with debris. A plume of dust swirls as hurried footsteps can be heard. A silhouetted figure comes stumbling in, coughing, and panting. At the sight of Zac's hat, the panting stops.

Gloved hands slowly reach out, but hesitate and draw back. Suddenly, they thrust forward and quickly snatch the iconic hat. Remaining in the shadows, the stranger tries Zac's hat on for size.

Fast approaching footsteps announce Danny's arrival. Looking about, he spots the silhouetted figure adjusting Zac's hat. He slowly reaches for his gun.

"Easy, cowboy."

Danny is surprised to hear a woman's voice. He rests a hand on his gun and asks, "Who are you?"

"Who's asking?" The stranger responds as she fusses with her new-found hat.

Not sensing her to be a threat, Danny concedes, "Colonel Briggs, Daniel Briggs. I'm Zac's chauffeur and body—"

Suddenly, two armor-clad, masked soldiers charge through the doorway, rifles at the ready.

One advances on Danny and inquires, "Dr. Gomes?"

Maneuvering next to Danny, the woman deftly shoves Zac's hat behind him and into his hands. Seeking to confirm their query, she gestures towards Danny. Unsure of what's happening, Danny plays along and nods.

"Sir, please come with us." The soldier's request is cordial but firm.

Bewildered, Danny leaves with the soldiers. As the stranger attempts to follow, her path is blocked by a soldier's outstretched arm.

"And just who might you be?"

She shoves the soldier's arm aside, and takes the lead. "Deanna, Deanna Jones."

Shocked by the declaration, Danny quickly mutters, "Jones? As in—"

"As in-Deanna Jones!" She sarcastically snaps her response as she muscles past Danny and the soldiers, who now stop, momentarily puzzled, before hurrying to catch up.

Moments later, the quietness of the chamber is interrupted by a jarring quake. The wall behind the Ark crumbles, partially revealing a Cross, resting on a huge, round stone. A faded but legible sign remains carved upon the Cross. It reads:

(*I am*) aleph vav tav
(*I am*) Alpha and Omega
(*I am*) God nailed upon the cross

EPILOGUE

After the Crucifixion

As proof of Jesus Christ's perfect sacrifice, God saw to it that all sacrificial rituals would no longer meet with His approval. Their failures continue to this day, thus proclaiming that Christ's death for the forgiveness of sin was truly *THE LAST SACRIFICE*.

These events, save the last, are found in both the Jerusalem and Babylonian Talmud.

- On the Day of atonement, God's approval of an offering was determined by lot, utilizing two stones, one white and one black. If the white stone was drawn, worthiness was indicated. *After the Crucifixion*, the black stone was forever drawn.
- At Yom Kippur, a crimson cord would miraculously turn white if the offering were deemed acceptable to God. *After the Crucifixion*, it never again turned white.
- *After the Crucifixion*, the 'rent' veil, whose tearing signified a new covenant and access to God, was replaced by massive doors that took 20 men to close. But every night, the doors opened of their

own accord. This lasted until the destruction of the Temple by the Romans.

- *After the Crucifixion*, the light from the three lamp shafts of the Menorah that indicated the blessing and presence of God failed to give their light, despite great effort to keep them lit.
- *After the Crucifixion*, Israeli's unending search for a red heifer continues to fail to produce one that meets all ritual requirements. (And they've been looking for two thousand years.)

This makes sense, in light of the fact that all sacrificial rituals were temporal, awaiting God, to provide, *to himself,** the perfect offering, *Jesus Christ, the lamb of God.***

*literal Hebrew translation, Genesis
22:8 KJV - ** John 1:29 KJV

———⟨ɘʋɘ⟩———

JESUS WAS NOT KILLED

https://afkimel.wordpress.com/2016/07/31/
the-god-man-who-could-not-die/

"Pilate marveled that He was already dead; and summoning the centurion, he asked him if He had been dead for some time." Mark 15:44 NKJV

Tertullian, Apol. XXI, noted of Jesus: "…And yet, nailed upon the cross, He exhibited many notable signs, by which His death was distinguished from all others. At His own free-will, He with a word dismissed from Him His spirit, anticipating the executioners work."

*"No one can take my life from me. I sacrifice it
voluntarily. For I have the authority to lay it down
when I want to and also to take it up again. For this is
what my Father has commanded."* John 10:18 NLT

Not until the appointed moment, did Jesus
Christ willingly surrender His life, with a

SHOUT!

And behold, the veil of the temple was torn in two
from top to bottom. — Matthew 27:51 NASB

And the earth did quake, and the rocks
rent; — Matthew 27:51 KJV

And the graves were opened; — Matthew 27:52 KJV

This why the hardened Roman Centurion Longinus, who
was a witness to these things, became a follower of Christ
and preached the good news of salvation. *This* is why he
accepted martyrdom, rather than flee, as his sympathetic
executioner's implored of him.

HalleluYAH!

WORKS CITED

THE UNTOLD CRUCIFIXION STORY
The Greatest Coverup in History

The story of YHVH being contextually translated: "Behold the hand! Behold the nail!" comes from Rabbi Yitzhak Kaduri. (The Rabbi the secret message and the Identity of Messiah, p.303, by Carl Gallups)

The conclusion regarding Christ's claim: "I am Alpha and Omega", can be translated as "aleph vav tav". Since "vav" has been translated as "nail" (by Rabbi Kaduri), it is my summation that although the book of Revelation (written in Greek) translates that Jesus declares, "I am Alpha and Omega", I believe that it should be read in Hebrew and taught as the profound proclamation that it was: "I am God nailed upon the cross".

Chapter 1

https://www.newdawnmagazine.com/articles/enoch-the-watchers-the-real-story-of-angels-demons

About the above website: Though riddled with questionable conclusions and baring an anti-Christian bias, some of the evidence revealed in this article can also be found in the Bible, the Dead Sea Scrolls as well as the apocryphal Book of Enoch.

Who are the Nephilim?
https://www.biblicalarcheology.org/daily/biblical-topics/
Hebrew-bible/who-are-the-nephilim/

Also: http://remnantreport.com/cgi-bin/imcart/read.cgi?article
id=165&sub=12

1. Researchers lost in Antarctica. https://www.foxnews.com/
science/russian-scientists-seeking-lake-vostok-lost-in-frozen-
land-of-the-lost

2. Several passageways leading deep into the earth exist, many with claims of alleged spirit/alien inhabitation and enlightenment. One lies beneath the Antarctic.
http://www.enterprisemission.com/antarctica.htm

Something's Going On Out There – by David Wimbish, ISBN 0-8007-5371-2 - (Aliens or Demons?)

3. A recent discovery of a city-sized anomaly under a massive frozen lake in the Antarctic.
https://www.express.co.uk/news/science/1082479/nasa-
antarctica-anomaly-frozen-city-lake-vostok-spt

This suggestion was put forth based on an accumulation of metals, which resembled the type of accumulations found in the ruins of ancient cities.

Chapter 2

4. The chromosome count was finally established by 1956.
http://www.nature.com/scitable/content/The-chrom osome-
number-in-humans-a-brief-15575/

Chapter 3

5. Basement gun ranges in high schools were common and safely operated for decades.
http://www.nationalreview.com/article/338167/
https://www.rallypoint.com/answers/school-gun-clubs-were-common-in-our-schools-in-the-1950-s-should-we-bring-them-back-and-familiarize-youths-with-the-discipline-of-shooting?cid=

Chapter 4

Israeli/Sinai war
www.historyguy.com/suez war 1956.html
Circus tent boxing
https://www.sheffield.ac.uk/nfca/researchandarticles/boxingbooth
Werewolf
http://militaryhistorynow.com/2015/10/23/the-fighting-werwolves-the-third-reichs-underground-army/
https://www.warhistoryonline.com/war-articles/operation-werwolf-nazi-plan-create-commando-force.html

Chapter 5

B-47, rocket assist take-off
http://www.lmstandish.net/Old-times/B-47 days.htm

Chapter 6

6. Confiscated B-17G – one of four covertly bound for Israel.
www.aerovintage.com/b17news1.htm

Shortly after the rebirth of Israel, four B-17's were secretly exported to aid in the creation of the Israeli Air Defense Force. One was seized in the Azores en route to Israel.

Chapter 7

The Rabbi the Secret Message and the Identity of the Messiah – by Carl Gallups p.66 Yeshua, the name of Jesus, means salvation.

Claim that the Ark of the Covenant has been discovered. http://www.bibleplus.org/discoveries/arkintro.htm/

1st Ark - Ex.25:10-22 / Ex.37:1-9 (1st set of broken tablets/commandments-manna-Aarons rod Heb.9:4) KJV

7. 2nd 'decoy' Ark (of the Covenant) was the one carried into battle and was never meant for sacrifices.
http://www.biblemysteries.com/library/arks.htm

The Ark of the Covenant was used to atone for sins, symbolically foreshadowing the great and final sacrifice of Jesus Christ. It remained in the encampment, while the second, decoy 'Ark' was the one carried into war.

2nd Ark - Deut.10:1-5 (2nd set of tablets/commandments only 1Kings8:9 / 2Chron.5:10) KJV.

Sacrificial blood sprinkled was said to have never touched the Ark but was caught up. https://sites.google.com/site/srolparishreligioused/eucharist-in-scripture

East side was for animal sacrifices, West side was reserved for the Messiah. http://www.remnantbride.com/Trinities/T-Part-7.htm

---

During missions, lead bombardiers fired a red flare to signal bombs dropped. http://www.hiredguns-hq.com/oldguns/linkspages/b17mission.htm

Chapter 8

Golgotha: *A Reconsideration of the Evidence for the Sites of Jesus' Crucifixion and Burial* by Joan Taylor (*Article published in the Spring 2002 issue of Bible and Spade.*)

8. Evidence that the real Ark of the Covenant lies beneath the Crucifixion site exists. Despite the controversy, this evidence addresses every theological proviso written about the Ark's true purpose.

GRATEFUL ACKNOELEDGMENT TO:
Wyatt Archeological Museum
A division of Wyatt Archeological Research, a non-denominational, non-profit, tax-exempt, 501 C3 research organization.
DISCOVERIES OF RON WYATT
Richard Rives, President of Wyatt Archeological Research
Board of Directors, Wyatt Archeological Research
Mary Nell Wyatt Lee
Eric Lembcke
Jerome Niswonger
Richard Rives
2502 Lynnville Hwy
Cornersville, TN 37047
Phone (931) 297-4745
www.archeology@united.net
www.wyattmuseum.com

Despite critics to the contrary, the Israeli Antiquities Authority had given Mr. Wyatts permission to conduct his excavation. Please see: https://www.arkdiscovery.com/iaa.htm

Also: https://wyattmuseum.com/the-ark-of-the-covenant-special-article/2011-338

Crucifixion site evidence http://webhome.idirect.com/~birkej/ark/arcofcov.htm/

The Alpha(Aleph) and Omega(Tav) are explained in a book entitled *The Rabbi the Secret Message and the Identity of the Messiah*, by Carl Gallups – p.46

Matthew 27:45 states that, during the Crucifixion, there was darkness over ALL the land. This claim was also confirmed by secular historians writing of the darkness in Rome, Greece, and Egypt. Among them, Eusebius, Julius Africanus, Maximus, Origen, Rufinus (Greek historian) and Phlegon.
http://www.christianhospitality.org/resources/first-church-rome-online/content/first-church-rome9.html

https://www.oxfordbiblechurch.co.uk/index.php/teachings/end-time-prophecy/763-the-day-the-sunstopped-shining

NASA confirmation of a blood moon occurring on April 3rd, 33 A.D. can be found at: https://www.bible.ca/archeology/jesus-christ-died-death-cross-eclipse-red-blood-moon-sun-darkness-earthquake-bodies-raised-resurrection-temple-veil-torn-in-two-centurian-son-of-god-3-april-33AD.htm#deatheclipse

Chapter 9

Stigmata, scent of jasmine
http://www.crystalinks.com/stigmata.html
http://saintscatholic.blogspot.com/p/stigmata-andstigmatist.html

Chapter 10

Atomic bomb test was an unofficial tourist attraction in the 1950's.
http://www.citylab.com/politics/2014/08/atomic-tests-were-a-tourist-draw-in-1950s-in-las-vegas/375802/

Hitler's Redoubt/Counterattack
http://www.nytimes.com/1964/08/02/hitlers-redoubtmenace-or-mirage.html?r=0

Sinatra: http://www.debbieschlussel.com/71226/exclusive-letter-details-secret-american-group-that-helped-israelbecome-a-state/

"Sultan of Swoon": One of Frank Sinatra's many Nicknames

Chapter 11

Retracting steps inspired by modern Japanese architecture book by Stephen Turnbull, Warriors of Medieval Japan, p. 183

The Aldebaran star system is found in the Taurus constellation.
http://www.space.com/22026-aldebaran.html

Isaiah 13:13 states that … *"the earth shall remove out of her place,…"* KJV. Some have speculated that the earth was moved on its axis, causing the sun to prematurely set, causing the stars to appear (though without luster) and the blood moon to prematurely rise, thus fulfilling prophecy and demonstrating the power and significance of the Son of God being crucified.

Dionysius and Appollophanes were in Egypt at the time of the Crucifixion. Both claimed to have watched the moon rise and align itself with the sun's vacated position! *That could explain the confusion about there being a solar eclipse during a full moon!* The hastened rotation of the earth would explain the pervasive

tremors. Dionysius and Appollophanes also reported that, after 3 hours, the moon, in retrograde, gave way to the sun as it returned.
http://www.christianhospitality.org/resources/first-church-rome-online/content/first-church-rome9.html

Phlegon, in his 13th book, wrote that in the 4th year of the 202nd Olympiad (A.D. 32-33 – *yes, the Olympics!*), "...an eclipse of the sun turned out to be the greatest of the known type prior, transforming the day at the sixth hour [noon] into such darkness of night that the stars could be seen in heaven, and the earth moved in Bithynia, toppling many buildings in the city of Nicaea."

Years later, historian, Pliny the elder (23-79 A.D.), wrote of a timekeeping Obelisk (i.e. sundial), being in error for decades. His reasoning first brought to mind a remarkable story circulating of the earth having been earlier displaced from its center.
Natural History xxxvi ch.15, p.335

The Alpha(Aleph) and Omega(Tav) are explained in a book by Carl Gallups entitled *The Rabbi the Secret Message and the Identity of the Messiah* – pp. 46 and 302

On the Possibility of Instantaneous Shifts of the Poles – by Flavio Barbiero
https://grahamhancock.com/barbierof1/

According to NASA, a lunar eclipse occurred on April 3rd, 33 A.D., the day of the Crucifixion.
https://eclipse.gsfc.nasa.gov/LEhistory/LEhistory.html

Bull's Eye coin (Fatimid coins)
http://www.antiquities.org.il/arch_coins_eng.aspx

Nephilim
https://www.biblicalarcheology.org/daily/biblical-topics/Hebrew-bible/who-are-the-nephilim/

9. Nazis, the occult, and the Aldebaran/Aryan race connection.

Nazis delved in occult practices often with terrifying results. Some entities, allegedly contacted, claimed to be from the Aldebaran star system. (AUTHORS NOTE: I know, hard to believe, but it's more a concern that Nazis believed it and acted on it! After all, we sent Pioneer 10 towards Aldebaran when there are stars much closer and at a time, after the war, when an ex-Nazi* was in charge at NASA.)
*https://en.wikipedia.org/wiki/Kurt_H._Debus
https://www.gaia.com/article/nazi-bell-ufo-technology

British in Antarctica – Operation Tabarin

Americans in Antarctica - National Geographic, Oct. 1947 issue

Allegedly proclaimed by Admiral Donitz at Nuremburg trial: "...invulnerable fortress, a paradise-like oasis in the middle of eternal ice." (Statement allegedly appears on this website)
http://www.bibliotecapleyades.net/tierra_hueca/esp_tierra_hueca15.htm

Authors Note:, After searching the 42-volume (Blue Series) transcripts of the Nuremberg trials, I failed to find Admiral Doenitz alleged claim, but I also noted a disclaimer stating that there were other, (excluded) transcripts. (Why would they be excluded?)

Chapter 12

After being confiscated in the Azores, the real-life fate of B-17G (44-83842) has become a matter of contention.

Chapter 13

https://www.quora.com/Was-Hitlers-goal-seriously-to-conquer-the-entire-world-and-exterminate-all-non-Aryan-races-How-on-earth-did-he-plan-to-achieve-that

10. A B-47 carrying two nukes was presumably lost at sea and never found (March 10, 1956)
http://www.aerospaceweb.org/question/weapons/q0268.shtml

Ascension Island (also known as "Wideawake Field"
http://www.ascension-island.gov.ac/aig/ascensionisland-about.htm

---

"He bowed the heavens also and came down with thick darkness under His feet" - 2Samuel22:10 (also: Psalm18:9 and Psalm144:5) KJV

"the God of Israel, who is enthroned above the cherubim" - 2Samuel6:2 (also: 2Kings19:15, Psalm80:1, Isaiah37:16) "the Lord's throne is in heaven" – Psalm11:4 (Ryrie Study Bible)

"the Lord is in His holy temple" – Psalm11:4 (NIV)

"And let them construct a sanctuary for Me, that I may dwell among them." – Exodus25:8 (also: Ex29:45,46, Num5:3, Deut12:11) KJV
Also see Deut. 31:6 *"He will never leave you."* KJV

"There I will meet with you, and from above the mercy seat, from between the two cherubim that are upon the ark of the testimony, I will speak with you..." – Ex25:22 KJV

The Ark of the Covenant is where heaven and earth met!

(read: The Apocalypse Code by Hank Hannegraaff p.216 and Jesus and the Victory of God, vol.2, Christian Origins and the Question of God by N.T. Wright (Minneapolis: Fortress, 1996), 205)

"And, behold, the veil of the temple was rent in twain from the top to the bottom; and the earth did quake, and the rocks rent;" Matthew 27:51 KJV

Also: The Gospel of Matthew and Its Readers: A Historical Introduction to the First Gospel (Bloomington: Indiana University Press, 2003) 238.

11. At Christ's death, a 4-fold message was instantly *'delivered'* with the 'renting' of the Temple veil (*Wow!*)

—The Temple veil was considered the Hem of Yahweh's Robe, His outer garment.

—Jewish tradition only allowed the father to 'rent' his outer garment during grief.

— "And Samuel said unto Saul, I will not return with thee: for thou hast rejected the word of the LORD, and the LORD hath rejected thee from being king over Israel. And as Samuel turned about to go away, he laid hold upon the skirt of his mantle, and it rent. And Samuel said unto him, *"The LORD hath rent the kingdom of Israel from thee this day, and hath given it to a neighbor of thine, that is better than thou."* 1Samuel 15:26-28 KJV.

—A remarkable story reports that Mary and others, were chosen by lot to help sew the veil 'rent' at the Crucifixion. https://www.thecompassnews.org/2012/08/some-stitches-in-time-with-the-mother-of-god/

Note: *I believe that the Father, in his compassion, chose Mary by lot to partake in the veils creation, to partake, in a real sense, in the rending of the veil (also known as the Hem of God's robe) upon the death of her earthly/divine son, Jesus Christ.*

12. The 3 hours of darkness, which occurred at the time of the Crucifixion, was a universal event documented by both Christ's followers and secular historians. (Yes, universal!!!!) https://creation.com/darkness-at-the-crucifixionmetaphor-or-real-history/

Arnobius, Contra Gentes I. 53: "But when, freed from the body, which He [Jesus] carried about as but a very small part of Himself [i.e. when He died on the cross], He allowed Himself to be seen, and let it be known how great He was, all the elements of the universe bewildered by the strange events were thrown into confusion. An earthquake shook the world, the sea was heaved up from its depths, the heaven was shrouded in darkness, the sun's fiery blaze was checked, and his heat became moderate; for what else could occur when He was discovered to be God who heretofore was reckoned one of us?"

In the apocryphal Gospel of Peter (v. 6), a great earthquake occurred just after Jesus expired and was taken off the cross and immediately before the reemergence of the sun.

In his Apologeticus, Tertullian wrote: *"at that same moment about noontide, the day was withdrawn; and they, who knew not that this was foretold concerning Christ, thought it was an eclipse. But this you have in your archives; you can read it there."* The foretelling is found in Amos 8:9 where it says: **"And it shall come to pass in that day, saith the Lord GOD, that I will cause the sun to go down at noon, and I will darken the earth in the clear day."**

Pontius Pilate sent a report to Tiberius Caesar in Rome: *"Now when he was crucified darkness came over all the world; the sun was altogether hidden, and the sky appeared dark while it was yet day, so that the stars were seen, though still they had their luster obscured, wherefore,*

I suppose your excellency is not unaware that in all the world they lighted their lamps from the sixth hour until evening. And the moon, which was like blood, did not shine all night long, although it was at the full, and the stars and Orion made lamentation over the Jews because of the transgression committed by them."

Acts 17: 6 sites that an angry mob searching for Paul and Silas, accused them of having "...**turned the world upside down**..." (Holman CSB)

Note: Taken figuratively, Acts 17:6 is hardly an accurate statement since the spreading of the Gospel had just begun. Taken literally, could be taken as further evidence that the Crucifixion was a physical, demonstrable, world-wide event. Also, it was not until the 13th century that the term, *'turned the world upside down'*, was officially recognized as a figurative expression.

Also, remember that historian Pliny the elder (23-79 A.D.) wrote of remembering a remarkable story circulating of the earth having been earlier displaced from its center. *Natural History* xxxvi ch.15, p.335

Chapter 14

(no citations)

Chapter 15

See: http://www.submarine-history.com/NOVAfour.htm/

13. A week after the war with Germany, the submarine U-234 surrendered. Among her cargo were found ten canisters of uranium oxide bound for Japan. (Used in the making of atomic bombs)

When it surrendered, German submarine U-234 it was found to be carrying, among other things, two Japanese officers and 1,200 pounds of uranium oxide. *New York Times* story by William J. Broad - Dec.31, 1995

Also see: https://www.h-net.org/reviews/showrev.php?id=4048

(Since 1941, Japan had been seeking to make its own atomic bomb but acquiring uranium had been a problem.)
See: www.atomicheritage.org/history/japanese-atomic-bomb-project

Bull's Eye stamp of Brazil (postage stamp)
https://en.wikipedia.org/wiki/Bull%27sEye

Operation Harvest Festival was a Nazi plan to shoot Jews, in a single event. In this case, 43,000.
http://hitlernews.cloudworth.com/occult-ahnenerbecastle-of-wewelsburg-tibet.php/
Ben Aharon's name: BEN-Right hand of God, AHARON-Light Bringer

Chapter 16

MOBY DICK was inspired by a real-life terror of the sea named Mocha Dick.
See: http://oceanservice.noaa.gov/facts/mobydick.html

Chapter 17

(no citations)

Chapter 18

British in Antarctica – Operation Tabarin

Chapter 19

(no citations)

Chapter 20

14. Saint Martin de Porres feast day is Nov. 3rd

15. Somatids (Microzymas) discovered by Dr. Pierre Jacques Antoine Bechamp.

Somatid: from the Greek word 'soma' meaning 'the body' and 'tidos' meaning 'he who creates.' (Also known as microzymas) www.pnf.org/compendium/Antoine Bechamp.pdf

See: http://anchorstone.com/chromosomes-somatids-and-the-blood-of-christ/

16. Some 'useful' Nazis found guilty at the Nuremberg trials were released and returned to their positions in the pharmaceutical cartel, a cartel condemned for war crimes! *Nuremberg trials condemned the executives of the pharmaceutical cartel.* See: END AIDS Break the Chains of Pharmaceutical Colonialism by Dr. Rath, p.151 – Dr. Rath Health Foundation

17. Nazis gathered by U.S. (including rocket scientists) after the war - Operation Paperclip. *Operation Paperclip was a covert program to import German scientists, engineers, and others whose former affiliation to the Nazi party was to be overlooked.* https://www.history.com/news/what-was-operation-paperclip

---

https://nypost.com/2016/12/29/massive-anomaly-lurks-beneath-ice-in-antarctica/

https://www.nasa.gov/missionpages/sunearth/news/mag-portals.html
https://www.pinterest.com/mrfreud/antarctica-whats-going-on-there/

Chapter 21

18. Nazi saboteurs - Operation Pastorius.
See: N.Y. Times July 4, 1942

The S.S. officer's speech is a compilation of several Nazi speeches and an excerpt from an article written by Margaret Sanger, the founder of Planned Parenthood, who once said, *"The most merciful thing that a large family does to one of its infant members is to kill it."* **Margaret Sanger, Women and the New Race (Eugenics Publ. Co., 1920, 1923)**

In her book, the Pivot of Civilization, Sanger wrote - *"...a part of a spawning class who should have never been born; and are human weeds to be exterminated."*

(These 3 sites bear repeating)

Hitler/Sanger
www.acts1711.com/sanger.htm/

Margaret Sanger and Nazi Party ties
also: http://www.acts1711.com/popcontrol.htm

The pseudo-science of eugenics
http://www.eugenics-watch.com/roots/chap13.html/

Chapter 22

(no citations)

Chapter 23

(no citations)

Chapter 24

"Ours is not to wonder why..." Based on a narrative poem by Lord Tennyson, Alfred 1854 – Charge of the Light Brigade

"Because I could not stop for death - Death kindly stopped for me." Based on a lyrical poem by Emily Dickinson entitled - "The Chariot"

Chapter 25

Shalom Zachor (remembering)
http://clarewynshul.co.za/vdvar.asp?p=622
Kaddish: "At some point, it's a mourner's duty to rise above personal pain and join others in a common venture,"
http://www.mishpacha.org/kaddish.shtml/

NEVER AGAIN, (slogan represents the Jewish people's resolve to never allow innocents to be brutalized for the crime of being Jewish)
https://www.algemeiner.com/2011/03/15/'neveragain'-is-not-just-a-slogan/

"Daphaq-daphaq!" (Hebrew for Knock-Knock)
https://www.rt.com/usa/341060-us-military-israeli -tactic-isis/
http://www.reuters.com/article/us-mideast-crisisusa-airstrike-idUSKCN0XN2NK/

Chapter 26

In 1964, a mystery all its own was the discovery of a fully stocked lifeboat abandoned on Bouvet Island, a frozen patch of land claimed to be the most isolated isle in the world, approx. 1,100 miles from Antarctica.

Chapter 27

(no citations)

Chapter 28

(no citations)

Chapter 29

NASA's FIRST DEEP SPACE PROBE, PIONEER 10 LAUNCHED FINAL DESTINATION: ALDEBARAN SYSTEM.

NASA - mission records were not archived – https://www.curiosity.com/topics/the-mystery-that-set-the-pioneerprobes-off-course-curiosity/

19. In 1979, an aging nuclear detection satellite recorded a nuclear blast on or near Antarctica. Despite the evidence, the U.S. denied the incident.

SATELLITE DETECTS NUCLEAR DETONATION IN ANTARCTIC –GOVERNMENT DENIES INCIDENT. http://www.nsarchive.gwu.edu/nukevault/ebb570-The22-September-1979-Vela-Satellite-Incident/ http://www.history-and-headlines.com/historyseptember-22-1979-vela-incident-ufo-or-secret-nuke-test/ http://www.gwu.edu/~nsarchiv/NSAEBB/NSAEBB 190/index.htm

20. NASA's 1ˢᵗ stellar traveler, Pioneer 10, is heading towards the Aldebaran star system. Who at NASA chose a destination that figured so prominently in Nazi ideology?
https://peoplepill.com/people/kurt-h-debus/

Author's Note: *I believe Pioneer 10's (launched July 15, 1972) destination (Aldebaran star system*) is evidence of Nazi ideology and its influence on the U.S. space program stemming from the influx of scientists from (Operation Paperclip) after World War II.* **Pioneer 10 was sent with the mission to make contact.** It is interesting to note that the first director of NASA was Kurt H. Debus, a former member of the Nazi party and Himmler's S.S. who was brought here under Operation Paperclip. Mr. Debus was director at the time of Pioneer 10's development and launch.

Chapter 30

Jewish tradition has it that after the ARK was built the builders were 'taken up' into heaven, lest their God-given skills would be used to build pagan idols.

Zac's disappearance is meant to reflect a similar fate, but as a reward bestowed him after a lifetime of service.

"I have fought the good fight, I have finished the race, I have kept the faith." 2 Timothy 4:7

Chapter 31

https://www.weekly.israelbiblecenter.com/hidden-hebrew-message-pilates-cross/

Also: The RABBI the SECRET MESSAGE and the Identity of MESSIAH - by Carl Gallups

EPILOGUE (References)

...God will provide himself, a lamb for
burnt offering...*Genesis 22:8 KJV

*This verse, which demonstrates Christ's deity, has been
unwittingly maligned by many versions of the Bible.
https://www.timefortruth.co.uk/content/pages/documents/
1351788556.pdf

Failure of rituals
Jerusalem Talmud "The Yerushalmi," p.156-157
Babylonian Talmud, Rosh HaShanah 31b, & Bavli, Tractate Yoma 39b:
https://www.pbs.org/wgbh/pages/frontline/shows/apocalypse/
readings/forcing.html

Sources for Israel eliminating its own alphabet (p.48) or YHVH
translating as Behold the Hand Behold the Nail (p. 303) *Please read*:
The RABBI the SECRET MESSAGE and the Identity of MESSIAH -
by Carl Gallups, ISBN 978-1-948014-12-0

Note: The trial of Jesus was the last held in the Sanhedrin chamber,
for it was destroyed 18 hours later by an earthquake.
http://www.spirit-digest.org/Quickhive%20articles/omens
tothejewsg.html

The rocks rent are visible to this day - See: **Benson Commentary**
on Matthew 27:51 (A supernatural event)

For a speculative commentary on the earth's rotation theory
involving the moon, go to:
http://www.christianhospitality.org/resources/first-church-
rome-online/content/first-church-rome9.html

NOTE: My belief is that, *if* God did choose to utilize the impact of a celestial body to 'rotate' the earth, I believe there is evidence that it may have involved impacting the earth rather than the moon, as others have speculated upon.. Recent scientific evidence shows that an asteroid/meteor impacted the earth during the Spring and in the Northern Hemisphere, coincidentally, the seasonal time and place of the Crucifixion!
https://www.nationalgeographic.com/science/article/dinosaur-killing-asteroid-most-likely-struck-in-spring

As incredible as it sounds, the suggested 'date' attributed to this event has cast even the idea of it being in error, beyond consideration. It is important to note that *ALL* such geographical dating methods have always demonstrated conflicting results and are extremely suspect.

Please read: *That Their Words May Be Used Against Them* by Henry M, Morris (This book contains over 400 pages with every page containing multiple examples of errors!)

Despite evidence, there remains a dispute as to whether there was a tetragrammaton. It was the Hebrew portion of Pilates sign, where the word 'and' becomes the key word in completing the tetragrammaton! The sign is alleged to still be in existence and that it clearly shows the Hebrew portion as appearing to have been rubbed away. Studies utilizing the Greek portion* suggest that the tetragrammaton was indeed there! *Pilates message was written in three languages.*

NOTE: Pilate had quite a habit of writing the conjunction, *and*. I counted 22 in just one of his paragraphs, with the next three paragraphs even beginning with *And*. Did God compel him or simply utilize Pilate's perchance for *and* to create the tetragrammaton?

NOTE: As incredible as it sounds, the accelerated, momentary rotation of the earth could have caused the reported quakes and destruction. This would give the appearance of the sun going down, as the blood moon rose to take the sun's place in the sky, *as reported*. This may explain the confusion (*Perhaps, also due to the momentary blinding due to the sudden darkness*) as to a solar eclipse being reported by some, *despite there being a full moon*! **There were far too many secular witnesses for anyone to simply dismiss all such claims.**

———❦❦❦———

*JESUS WAS NOT KILLED

"Pilate marveled that He was already dead; and summoning the centurion, he asked him if He had been dead for some time." Mark 15:44 NKJV

Tertullian, Apol. XXI, noted of Jesus: "...He Himself had predicted this, which, however, would have signified little had not the prophets of old done it as well. And yet, nailed upon the cross, He exhibited many notable signs, by which His death was distinguished from all others. At His own free-will, He with a word dismissed from Him His spirit, anticipating the executioners work."

The Roman orator Cicero called crucifixion "a most cruel and ignominious punishment," "the most miserable and most painful punishment appropriate to slaves alone." https://www.vision.org/crucifixion-and-the-real-cause-of-jesus-death-2818

During crucifixion, one could freely inhale but not exhale. To avoid suffocation, the crucified bore the brutal task of lifting one's body to exhale, each time bearing the agonizing pain of pulling against the spikes driven through the median nerve in the upper forearms. This is what made Christ's final, some say supernatural, victory shout so remarkable.

"No one can take my life from me. I sacrifice it voluntarily. For I have the authority to lay it down when I want to and also to take it up again. For this is what my Father has commanded." John 10:18 NLT

Not until the appointed moment, did Jesus
Christ willingly surrender His life, with a

*SHOUT!**

And behold, the veil of the temple was torn in two
from top to bottom. — Matthew 27:51 NASB

And the earth did quake, and the rocks
rent; — Matthew 27:51 KJV

And the graves were opened; — Matthew 27:52 KJV

This why the hardened Roman Centurion Longinus, who was a witness to these things, became a follower of Christ and preached the good news of salvation. *This* is why he accepted martyrdom, rather than flee, as his sympathetic executioner's implored of him.

HalleluYAH!

*Jesus cried out again in a *loud* voice (Matt. 27:50) and died – *loud* = megas = G3173 = high, large, loud, mighty, strong - Strong's Concordance

https://www.themoorings.org/Jesus/crucifixion/cause of death. html

https://www.theguardian.com/science/2004/apr/08/thisweeks
sciencequestions
https://www.legacyicons.com/saint-longinus-the-centurion...

"For as Jonas was three days and three nights in the whale's belly; so shall the Son of man be three days and three nights in the heart of the earth." Matt. 12:40 KJV

'3 days and 3 nights' was an idiom peculiar to the Hebrew language. When translated into Greek, it becomes clear that this 'figure of speech' was to be understood as one whole day, since both night, and day constituted the whole, and a portion of two others.

The Babylonian Talmud bears this out by stating that a "portion of a day is as the whole of it."

Since a day began with the evening, I believe a great oversight may be the failure to consider the 3 hours of darkness as a portion of the 3 day/ night phenomenon.

Good Friday

Darkness from 12 P.M. to 3 P.M. (*Night one*).
3 P.M. 'til 6 P.M., the sun 'returned' (*Day one*).
6 P.M. 'til 6 A.M. (*Night two*) and 6 A.M. 'til 6 P.M. (*Day two*)
This completed the only whole day, Saturday.
6 P.M. (*Night three*) began *the third day* (Christ's resurrection could have occurred at any moment after 6 P.M. as the idiom, *three days and three nights,* was thus fulfilled.)
Again, as stated, a "portion of a day is as the whole of it."

For further reading on the subject, go to: https://hermeneutics. stackexchange.com/questions/21512/do-idioms-used-in-the-crucifixion-narrative-resolve-the-3-day-3-night-objectio

Printed in the United States
by Baker & Taylor Publisher Services